THE YARBOROUGH BRAND

Seth Yarborough returned to the JayBar spread after six years, hoping to clear himself with his father, J.B. Yarborough, who believed Seth had killed his older brother Jeremy in cold blood. Now Seth had come to claim his own. But he came back to find a deadly ambush waiting for him . . .

THE YARBOROUGH BRAND

Lee Hoffman

GUNSMOKE

First published by Robert Hale, Ltd.

This hardback edition 2002
by Chivers Press
by arrangement with
Golden West Literary Agency

ISBN 0 7540 8169 9

British Library Cataloguing in Publication Data available.

Printed and bound in Great Britain by
BOOKCRAFT, Midsomer Norton, Somerset

To Redd Boggs

for Radcliffe and Merriweather

Chapter 1

He drew rein at the edge of the grass and sat looking at the house silhouetted against the night sky.

Damn, but it was big. A brick mansion with galleries running the width of both stories and thick white columns rising from ground to roof. There were mullioned windows, a couple of them showing the glow of lamplight through lace curtains. *Mansion* was the word all right. It looked like a New Orleans whorehouse.

Touching his spurs lightly to the horse's flanks, he walked it along the curved gravel drive that swept between neat-cropped hedges. Plenty fancy for a high-country beef ranch. At the steps he paused, gazing at the house again, wondering. Then he swung stiffly out of the saddle and let the reins fall. There was a cast-iron post but he ignored it, leaving the horse ground-hitched. Might be he'd want to leave fast.

No, he told himself. He ran a hand along the coyote-dun's neck, feeling the caked sweat and dirt. Through his fingers, he could feel the animal's weariness. A good horse, but run out now. The horse wouldn't be able to run much farther without rest and a decent feed.

He rubbed a hand over his own face, thinking he was about run out himself.

As he started toward the steps, the gravel crunched under his boots and his spurs jangled. It sounded too loud in the night. He told himself it probably couldn't be heard in the house, but he pulled off the spurs and slung them over the saddle horn. Tense and cautious, he climbed to the gallery and walked toward one of the lit windows. From somewhere deep inside the building, he could hear the faint sound of a piano. Like a New Orleans whorehouse, he thought again as he neared the window.

It was open. Through the curtains, he could see the room clearly. It was a study, the walls paneled with warm

7

dark wood. The shaggy head of a bull buffalo was mounted over the fireplace.

That glowering bull's head had been in the old house too. But it was the only thing in the room that looked familiar. The rest of it—shelves with leather-bound books, a huge mahogany desk littered with papers and ledgers, a wingbacked chair angled away from the window—none of these had come from the old place.

The old house had been plenty big enough, he thought darkly. Too big a lot of the time. Tallow lamps had never quite been able to light away the shadows in it. Boot heels had sounded too loud on the bare plank floors. Even the stone hearth and the big iron range in the kitchen hadn't been able to drive out the chill that would linger in its corners. He wondered if this elegant mansion was any warmer.

Only one lamp burned in the wood-paneled study. It sat on a little table next to the winged chair. Its chimney was clean, and the bright-polished brass of its base reflected its flame. But it failed to reach into the room's dark corners.

Beside the lamp, a cut-glass decanter caught sparks of light in its facets and the depths of the brandy it held. The round-bellied glass beside it was empty. That was different too. The old man used to slug his liquor from the bottle.

He couldn't see the man in the chair from where he stood—only the outstretched legs and the polished, hand-tooled yellow boots crossed at the ankles. Expensive boots. Big boots for a big man.

He stood there, stiff-shouldered, gazing through the window, deciding that he was certain who was in the chair and that the man was alone. But even after he'd decided, he hesitated. He knew damned well this wasn't going to be an easy thing to do.

Finally, he swung a leg over the windowsill and stepped into the room. The feel of his boot heels sinking deep into the pile of the carpet startled him. For an instant it had seemed like there was nothing solid under his feet.

It took a moment for the man in the chair to realize that someone had come into the room. Stirring from his drowsing, he turned toward the window. He squinted incredulously at the figure framed against it, shocked that anyone would dare come in on him that way.

8

The intruder looked like a cowhand. A down-luck, grub-line rider from the way he was dressed. Certainly not one of *his* hired hands. Young, lean-built, not very tall, with an unshaven jaw and road dust all over his clothes. Damned impudent pup to come tromping in through a window that way, uninvited and unannounced. He glanced at the gun tied low on the intruder's thigh, then looked again toward the face that was lost in shadows, partly hidden by the hat brim cocked down over it.

"What the hell do you mean coming through my window like that?" he demanded.

"Pa?" the intruder said thinly.

Startled, the old man peered at him as he pushed back the hat and took a slow step closer. The lamplight caught his face then.

"Seth."

"I've come back, Pa." His voice was stiffly defiant. He gazed intently at the old man, but he could see no reaction. Not the twitch of a muscle. Coldly, he added, "Or should I say *Mister* Yarborough? Do I know you well enough to call you J.B.?"

The old man's face tightened subtly, his eyes narrowing a trace, his mouth hardening. "Why have you come back?"

"Why not?" Seth Yarborough said. The old man hadn't changed at all, he thought as he studied that strong-boned, hard-weathered face. The thick hair that must once have been a stark black was streaked with gray. So were the heavy brows and full moustaches. But that was the way Seth remembered him. J.B. would be well into his sixties now, but he looked no more than a rawhide fifty.

The eyes that held steady on Seth were the same as he remembered them too. Dark, narrowed under a perpetual frown marked by deep squint-lines from years under bright suns. Eyes as veiled as a rattlesnake's. No, the old man hadn't changed at all.

"You were *told*," J.B. answered him. "When you left you were told to get and stay got."

Seth shrugged. "Hell, after six years, I figured maybe . . ."

"*You* figured! *I'm* the head of this damned . . ." the old man stopped himself. Raising a hand, he gestured vaguely, as if he groped for something. Then he pointed toward the footstool. "Sit down."

It was an order and Seth obeyed it. He seated himself on the edge of the ottoman.

9

"Take off your hat in my house."

He did, setting it on the table. He hadn't realized until then, when he put it on the mirror-bright surface of polished mahogany, just how shabby the old Stetson was. He looked at his boots, suddenly seeing them as deep-scuffed and badly worn. His Levi's were faded almost gray and about to tear through at the knees. He knew his shirt wasn't much better.

These were the things his father was seeing about him, he thought. These were what the old man would judge him by—the ragged clothes, the road dirt, the unshaven face. He let his eyes rest on his boot toes.

"You're in trouble again," J.B. said. It wasn't a question. Seth nodded.

"You think I'll get you out of it." Another cold and certain statement.

"Not *me*," Seth snapped. "But maybe the Yarborough name. Maybe you wouldn't cotton much to seeing the family name in the newspapers. Something like *son of J. B. Yarborough, prominent Long County rancher, hanged for murder . . .*"

"Murder!" The old man got to his feet. He stood tall, well over six feet even without the Mexican boots that added to his height. And he was broad, thick through the chest and full-shouldered. He seemed to loom over Seth. "Of all the damn fool . . . *murder?*"

Seth nodded, still gazing at his own boots.

Turning away from him, J.B. drew a deep breath, then muttered, "Well, you've always been headed that way, haven't you? Looking to end yourself up on a rope sooner or later."

"Maybe *you* should have hanged me. A nice quiet family affair!"

"You know I never believed . . ."

"Like hell you didn't!"

"Seth, I . . ."

"You ran me out. And now I reckon you're wondering where I get the gall to keep using the Yarborough name."

"It's the name *I* gave you," the old man said.

"You know how much I care about it. But if I'm gonna drag any name through the mud, it'll be Yarborough. If they hang me, it'll be as J. B. Yarborough's son. I'll make damn sure of that. Unless *you* want to tell them different!"

With tense deliberation, J.B. pulled the stopper from the

10

decanter. He poured a little brandy into the glass and drank it. Then he turned to look at Seth again. With resignation, he said, "*Maybe* I can square it. Where did it happen?"

"Across the line a ways. Town called Horseshoe, in Kansas."

"That's in Spence County, isn't it? Trail town?"

Seth nodded.

"Who'd you kill?"

"Man name of Wilson. He worked in a saloon."

Nodding to himself, J.B. muttered, "I can go in and see Grayling tomorrow . . ."

"You want to know how it happened?" Seth asked sharply.

"Does it matter?"

"You care *why* it happened?"

J.B. looked at the gun on Seth's thigh and then at his face—at the narrowed eyes and hard-set mouth. As if he read all that he wanted to know there in that face, he shook his head.

"Verdict of murder," Seth said. "That's a majority vote, ain't it? Judge and jury agreed unanimously?"

Anger flared behind J.B.'s eyes. Viciously, he snapped back, "Do you *sell* your gun now? Or do you just kill for the fun of it?"

"Good God, Pa, you don't know . . . !"

"I know *you*, Seth. Near nineteen years I raised you. And I can see six more years ain't changed you any. You're older now, and shabbier, but I don't see any other difference."

"A hundred dollars and a horse don't . . ."

"That's more than *I* had when I started. You think you've been cheated? You think I owed you more than the money and the horse I gave you? You think just because . . ."

"I don't think *anything!* I stopped thinking a long time ago."

"You never did any thinking. Never used your damned head. I bought you out of scrapes—tried to beat some sense into you." The old man's voice sank deep into his throat, like an animal growl. "I thought maybe, after I buried Jeremy, I thought— Seth, I gave you the money and the horse and I—" Whatever he meant to say, he didn't finish it.

11

Instead, drawing a deep breath, he snapped angrily, "But now you're back like this, on your knees to me, begging me to get your neck out of a noose!"

"I ain't on my knees!"

"You damn well should be!"

Moving with awkward stiffness, Seth got to his feet. His fingers were so tense that they almost trembled as he reached for the hat. "You gonna come to the hanging? Maybe cheer a bit—*to hell with Seth Yarborough!*"

"You bastard!"

Seth swung.

He meant to hit—to ram his fist into that stone-hard face. He felt the hand move, then jerk back against his will. It halted short of landing the blow. And he felt an overwhelming sense of futility. It had always been that way. He could holler back at the old man, could curse him with every damned hard name ever thought of—but he couldn't *hit* back.

As J.B. ducked away from the blow, his hands went to the buckle of the wide leather belt he wore. A quick tug stripped it from around his waist. He swung it double in his hand.

Seth jumped. He backed as the old man lashed out with the belt. One step, another, and then he felt the wall, unyielding at his shoulders. He threw up both hands, trying to shield his face as J.B. struck out. He caught the stinging blows on his arms. The old man swung that belt like a damned bullwhip.

He tried to grab it. He'd tried that before, too, long ago. Only he'd never managed to catch it before. This time his fingers closed over it.

He jerked. Wrapping both hands around the belt, he tried to wrench it loose from J. B.'s grip. But the old man was too strong. He couldn't pull it away. For a long moment they stood braced, both pulling against the belt they clung to.

"Goddammit!" Seth heard himself shout. "Ain't you satisfied yet?"

And suddenly he was falling back against the wall with the belt free in his hands. J.B. had let it go.

Wheeling away from Seth, the old man stalked across the room and jerked open the door. Wordlessly, without looking back, he slammed it shut behind him.

Seth stared at the door. Then he flung the belt. It

thudded against the door panels and fell to the floor. Looked like a dead snake lying there, he thought. He rubbed his hands over his arms, where he'd caught the thrashing. No, not dead yet—it still had a damn hard bite. Did anything that vicious ever die?

Slapping the hat onto his head, he left the room the way he'd come in—through the window. He gathered reins and rose wearily to the saddle. For a while, he just sat there on the coyote dun, gazing at the house. Hell of a place. But there wasn't anywhere else to go, was there?

He gigged the horse into motion, swinging around the house. In the pale moonlight, he scanned the other buildings of the ranch. It was easy enough to pick out the different sheds and the bulk of the barn. The low silhouette with squares of dim-lit windows would be the bunkhouse. All were set well away with a wide back yard separating them from the big house. And the corrals were even farther away, all downwind as if J.B. didn't want any taint of stable smells drifting up to his mansion.

Keep it pure and clean, Seth thought as he headed for the corrals. Keep any stink away from the Yarborough house. And keep any stink off the Yarborough name, too, you sonofabitch.

He stripped the dun and loosed it into the corral. Groping in the darkness, he located a scoop of corn from the feed shed. Then he fetched an armload of hay. By the time he'd dumped it in the corral, the dun had rolled. A good horse, he thought again. But even a strong hard cayuse had to stop and rest sometime.

He jerked the tie-strings and pulled the bedroll off his saddle. The barn would be as good a place as any to bed down. Good as he'd find around here, he figured. Slinging the bundle over his shoulder, he started for it.

A door opened suddenly in the back end of the bunkhouse. It spilled lamplight, silhouetting the man who stood in the doorway.

"Who is that? Who's messing around out there?"

The familiar voice startled Seth. He called, "Mace? You're still here?"

There was no answer. Not until he'd stepped into the spill of light. Then, sounding as if he couldn't quite believe it, Mace said, "Seth? It's really you?"

Seth grinned. "No, it's some other damned bastard."

"Hell, come on in."

The room hung onto the back end of the bunkhouse was the foreman's quarters. As Seth walked into it, he asked, "You're ramrod here now?"

Mace nodded in reply. "So you come back. Set while I boil some coffee. Sorry I ain't got anything stronger. How've you been? What . . . ?" He cut his question short, looking embarrassed by whatever he'd almost asked.

"What the hell brings me back here?" Seth offered, glancing around. The room was small, crowded by the big brass bedstead piled high with featherbeds, an iron stove, a small table with a lone chair set to it, and a massive store-bought bureau. The mirror over the bureau showed him back his own image.

"Yeah," Mace said. "Does J.B. know you're here?"

Seth gazed at his own reflection. Slowly he said, "Yeah, I talked to him already." Then, rubbing at his still-stinging arms, he amended it. "*He* talked to *me*."

Mace was busying himself with the coffeepot. He kept his back turned as he asked, "You home to stay now?"

"What do you think?" Seth snorted. He drew his eyes away from his image and settled into the chair.

Turning, the foreman looked him down curiously. Seth knew Mace was seeing him the way the glass had just shown him to himself, shabby and dirty. Self-consciously, he rubbed his knuckles across the stubble on his jaw. Hell of a long way from the flash dandy he'd seen in mirrors six years ago.

"You look tired," Mace said.

"Yeah," he mumbled, thinking that was a charitable way of putting it.

"Long ride?"

"Six years is a hell of a long ride."

Mace shot a questioning glance toward the bedroll. "You're gonna be here a while?"

"Not sure. I was just about to pick myself a stall and bed down in the barn for the night."

"You ain't sleeping in the big house?"

"Under *his* roof?"

"It's still that way?"

"Yeah."

Mace turned his back again. "Hell of a thing," he grunted. "Why don't you spread your soogans in here? Take one of the featherbeds. It gets chilly in the barn come morning."

"Thanks." Seth stretched out his legs and looked at his boots. He could feel some of the stiffness easing out of his shoulders. It would be more comfortable camping here in Mace's quarters. More comfortable in a lot of ways. He repeated, "Thanks."

Mace muttered something he couldn't quite make out and hurried to look after the coffee. Embarrassed by the thanks, Seth thought. And by the reason for it—the damned awkward situation. Mace had been a friend. Still was one. He felt grateful that there was somebody here he could take refuge with. Coming back—especially this way—hadn't been easy.

Mace had been on the Yarborough place ever since the old man decided to turn his holdings into cattle land. He had come up the trail with that first herd J.B.'d brought in from Texas. He'd stayed to settle them in, to work them and now to be foreman of the JayBar spread. Seth wondered why he'd been surprised that Mace was still here. Mace would always be here. It was where he belonged.

Looking at him now, Seth wondered at the way six years seemed to have aged him so much more than they had J.B. Mace couldn't be forty yet, but his hair was going from pitch-black to dull gray and his shoulders had begun to slope as if he were weary from a long burden. He didn't seem quite as tall as Seth remembered him either, but that might be because he was wearing moccasins now instead of boots.

Mace seemed uncomfortable in the moment of silence. He broke it, asking, "Where've you been?"

"Texas, New Mex, Kansas—places," Seth muttered. Mace was holding back, and he figured he knew what the unasked questions were. But he didn't feel like answering them. Not now. Right now he was too tired to talk much about anything. Especially not important things.

Mace made another jab at conversation. "Been working cattle?"

"Yeah. Mostly uptrail to the railroad."

"Like it?"

"It's a job."

Mace picked up the coffeepot. As he poured, Seth looked at his face. The dark skin and wide cheekbones showed part Indian blood.

Did the Yarboroughs have Indian blood, he wondered.

15

They weren't so dark, but their bone was strong in that same way, and their hair tended toward the same kind of coarse black. That is, all the Yarboroughs except him. He ran a hand through his own hair, pushing it back off his forehead.

Mace was gazing at him, seeming to cast about for something else conversational to say. But there were too many other thoughts bothering the foreman. He blurted out, "He's married again, you know."

"I heard," Seth said, trying to sound as if it didn't matter. He shrugged in the direction of the big house, "I s'pose he built that place for *her*?"

"Yeah, he tore the old one to the ground after . . . after . . ."

"Hell, say it. I'm used to it by now," he grunted. But he knew it wasn't true. Coming back here had been like walking back through time. For six years he'd shied clear of the memories, fighting them until he'd thought they were dead. But now—here—they were all alive again and as sharp as fresh-honed knives.

"After he run you off," Mace finished slowly, his eyes intent on Seth. "He tore the old place down then and moved into town. Wasn't till after he started courting her that he set in to building again."

"What kind of woman is she?"

"Handsome. Young, too. Hell, she's younger'n me. A blond-headed woman, like your mother was, only not so tall and strong."

Startled, Seth asked, "You knew my mother? You never told me that before."

Mace nodded reluctantly.

"But I thought she was dead when you came here."

Mace twined his fingers together and stared at them, looking uncertain. After a moment, he said, "I kinda knew her down to Texas before J.B. married her. But she was already dead when I come up here and I didn't see no point in talking about her. I didn't rightly ever *know* her. I was only just a kid then—only just had seen her around to know who she was."

It still seemed strange he'd never mentioned her before, Seth thought. He asked, "What kind of woman is this number three Mrs. Yarborough?"

"She ain't a woman for *working* on a place, the way your mother was. She's more the kind for looking at and

16

keeping care of and . . . Hell, you ought to see her when she's done up, Seth. The old man had a party here not long back and everybody come to it. The governor himself and all kinds of bigwigs from Denver, and she fit right in with them all, gossiping with their womenfolk and everything."

What did they gossip about, Seth wondered. It would sure raise a helluva gossip among those gold-plated friends of J.B.'s if the old man's son got himself hanged for murder, wouldn't it? They probably talked behind his back now about how he'd had a wife that cheated on him and gave him a boy with the Yarborough name but not the Yarborough blood. But that was still just gossip. J.B. had never owned to it in public.

If it came to a trial though, the old man would have to make his choice. He could deny one, but by doing it, he'd be admitting the other: Either his second wife had been a cheat or his second son a murderer.

And J.B. wouldn't cotton to that at all, Seth told himself. The old man would pull every last string and grease every last palm he could to keep that from happening. He was probably sitting up right now, worrying how to take care of that murder warrant. Maybe he wouldn't sleep too easy tonight, either.

Seth grinned at the thought as he rubbed his hands over his arms. They still hurt from that whipping.

Chapter 2

Seth woke before dawn. Remembering where he was, he turned over and went back to sleep. He woke again at the sound of Mace's voice.

"Seth?"

"Huh?" He sat up and rubbed at his face, then looked questioningly at the foreman.

Mace was dressed. Looked like he'd been up and around a while already. But then the foreman's day on JayBar began almost as early as a drover's on the trail.

"I've been talking to J.B.," Mace was saying, his voice heavy with significance.

"About me?"

"Yeah. He just left. Said to tell you he's gone to town to see that lawyer, Grayling. Said you should know why. He expects he'll be gone overnight and says you should stay close on JayBar land—not show your face around till he's got things settled."

Seth yawned and stretched his shoulders. So he'd been right: The old man would pay off to protect the family name. He wasn't surprised. But he didn't feel pleased or relieved either and that seemed strange.

"What kind of trouble?" Mace asked.

"Nothing much."

"J.B. seemed right upset about it."

"I reckon it'll cost him a fair piece of money to get this one straightened out," he mumbled. It occurred to him he really owed Mace some kind of an explanation of what was going on. Tersely, he added, "Shooting scrape over in Kansas."

"*Again?*"

The word seemed to have slipped out without Mace's intending it, but it still struck sparks. Seth snapped back, "Dammit, I was never in *that* much trouble!"

Mace eyed him. "Weren't you?"

18

He bit back a sharp answer. Instead, he protested, "Not *gun* trouble, Mace. Mostly it was just brawling and hoorawing."

"Except the last time," Mace said slowly.

It sounded deliberate. It sounded like he *meant* to prod. But that didn't make sense. Seth struggled back the rising anger, telling himself that in six years he'd learned at least one thing besides droving. He'd learned that he had to keep a tight rein on his temper if he wanted to hold a job and keep eating. Now he'd better hold onto it if he wanted to keep a friend—the only friend he had around this place.

He gazed a moment longer at Mace, wondering what to say now. Then he shrugged. Stretching out on the quilt, he closed his eyes. Maybe if he just kept his mouth shut— maybe if he ignored the impending trouble, it would go away.

When he was sure that Mace had left the room, he let his eyes open again. He lay staring at the ceiling, thinking how close he'd come to really throwing hard words. And maybe worse. Why the hell did he have to get rankled and proddy with Mace? Hadn't that scene with J.B. last night been enough to satisfy the devils that drove him?

When he finally got up, he found the fire still burning and the coffeepot half full. It had been shoved to the back of the stove to wait for him. He pulled it over the fire again, feeling worse guilty about that near scrap with Mace. Why the hell did things like that happen?

He poured out a cup and settled at the table, wondering what would happen if he went up to the big house looking for breakfast? If he ran into J.B.'s new wife, he'd likely end up in some kind of unpleasantness with her, too. Well to hell with that. The idea of chousing up a meal at the cookshack didn't seem very promising either. The hands probably knew all the talk, would probably know who he was.

He decided he wasn't hungry enough to bother with breakfast anyway. He gulped down the rest of the coffee, then looked outside.

The place seemed uncommonly still. As he headed to the pump to fetch water, he could spot a couple of men working over at the fenced pasture. But they were a good way off. Didn't seem to be anyone at all around the barn or the bunkhouse. He wondered if Mace had sent them all to chores at a distance so they wouldn't run into him. Afraid he was so damned touchy he'd get into trouble with them too?

He took the water back into the foreman's room and set it over the fire. There was no reservoir on this stove. He had to heat it in the bucket. As he waited, he stripped and looked over his arms.

That thrashing had raised welts. Hell of a thing to take a strapping like that—like a dumb kid. Why hadn't he been able to hit back? Was he afraid of the old man?

He shaved and then scrubbed thoroughly. The hot water was a welcome luxury. It would have been good to loaf in a tub full of it for a while, soaking some of the soreness out of his arms and the weariness out of his bones. But there wasn't any tub in the foreman's quarters. Likely there was a real fancy one somewhere in that big house. But damned little difference that made to him.

Standing in front of the mirror, he looked himself over. Shaving and washing had helped. Critically, he studied the face that gazed back at him. The bone was light and sharp, the jaw thin, the nose almost straight, barely showing the damage of having been broken. The eyes had a narrow set and the mouth a hard line.

He decided that it was a mean face. He'd heard that said a few times. The idea didn't bother him. Hell, he'd worked at it. If a man looked ornery enough people tended to leave him be. And that was what he'd asked of the world—for the last six years at least—that it leave him be.

He wondered how much his face had changed since he was a kid. Back then the people who'd known her had said he looked like his mother. *That* hadn't been anything to start an argument about. The trouble hadn't been so much with his face, but with his build and hair.

His mother had been lithe, but tall and so blond that from a distance she looked white-haired. And J.B. was tall, big-boned, almost as dark as an Indian. But Seth Yarborough had stopped growing about four inches too short and easy forty pounds too light—for a Yarborough.

He ran a hand through hair that was a dirty-clay red. There never had been a red-headed Yarborough, and Yarboroughs *always* bred true. He'd heard that over and over when he was a kid. No Yarborough would throw a scrawny red-haired whelp, they said. Then who did, he wondered.

He beat as much of the dirt as he could out of the Levi's and shirt before he put them on again. They felt stale and uncomfortable against clean skin. But they were what he had.

A hundred dollars and a horse.

He supposed he could have done something a damn sight better with those gold eagles than throw them away across a bar. Only it was too late to start thinking about that now. Too late to start thinking at all.

Pausing in the doorway, he studied the back of the big house. Even from the rumpside, it was elegant. Broad galleries with whitewashed railings that looked starkly clean against the dark-red brick of the walls, curtained windows, flowerbeds—even from this side it looked like a New Orleans whorehouse. He wondered if the new Mrs. Yarborough happened to be home.

Jamming his hands into his pockets, he started toward the corrals. What the hell was he going to do with himself while he was stuck here? He sure didn't feel like lending a hand with the ranch work.

He looked at the coyote dun. That ride had gaunted it. Little rest and feed would cure that though. With a sigh he hoisted himself up onto the top fence rail and began idly to build a cigarette. As he licked it closed, he glanced at the house again.

Had that been a face at the window suddenly drawing away? Had somebody been looking at him from behind those curtains? The new Mrs. Yarborough maybe? He imagined she'd be right curious about him.

He lit the cigarette, watching the house from the corner of his eye. The back door edged open a bit. Somebody hesitated just inside, then shoved it open and stepped onto the gallery.

It was a boy, maybe sixteen or so, dressed in riding clothes. Not a ranch hand's clothes though. Those neat, expensive britches and that silk shirt, the sharp-creased belly Stetson and bright-polished boots weren't meant for working in.

The kid seemed uncertain. He paused, then squared his shoulders and started down the steps. With studied determination, he headed toward the corrals, striding long and

21

hitting the ground hard with each step. His fancy spurs rang like bells.

There was a gun on his hip, in a tooled holster that was set low and tied down. Looked like carved ivory butts on the revolver. Seth wondered how much an outfit like that would set a man back these days. Likely a damn sight more than a good using horse.

The kid was tall, light-boned and thin, but with a softly pudgy look to his face, as if he still had a layer of baby fat under his skin. A little hard work would have changed that, Seth thought as he watched the boy striding toward him. At that age some kids were close onto being men. From the look of him, this one might be trying, but he just wasn't making it.

The hat was cocked down over the boy's forehead and his chin outthrust. He stopped in front of Seth and leaned back his head to peer up from under the hat brim.

Seth felt a little like grinning. But he returned the boy's gaze with cold and steady eyes.

The kid blinked first.

His voice a little too loud, more tense than hard, he said, "You're *Seth*, ain't you?"

"Yeah."

"I'm Charles Yarborough."

No trace of his surprise showed in Seth's face. He'd heard about the third Mrs. Yarborough, but not this. Edging his voice with skepticism, he said, "Yarborough?"

The boy blinked again. But he stood firm. "Charles O'Connor *Yarborough*."

"They call you Chuck or Charlie?"

He was obviously taken aback. It sure wasn't the response he'd expected. Sounding as though he thought maybe Seth hadn't understood, he said, "I am the son of Mrs. Lucille Yarborough."

"So J.B. got himself a stepson, eh?" Seth muttered. "Funny I never heard about you."

"*I've* heard plenty about *you!*" The words were knife-sharp. It sounded as if nothing he'd heard had been good.

"From J.B.?" Seth asked.

"No. He doesn't talk about you at all. But I've heard plenty."

"Where?"

The kid hesitated. Evasively, he answered, "Around. Around the bunkhouse."

22

Seth wondered just how fancy the gossip could have gotten during these past six years. It had been fancy enough to begin with. He shifted his weight, feeling uncomfortable under the boy's gaze. "So you're heir to the throne now?"

"Huh?"

"You expect all this will be yours one of these days?" He gestured toward the house, the outbuildings, the meadow and the mountains.

Charles O'Connor Yarborough nodded slowly, his eyes wary.

Seth forced a grin, knowing it came out mean and humorless. "Funny the way things can work out to change a feller's plans. You know, I had a notion like that once myself."

"Only you're not really a Yarborough!"

He couldn't hold the imitation of a grin any longer. He gave up trying and mumbled, "Another county heard from."

"Huh?"

"Democracy. Majority vote carries."

The kid looked completely bewildered by that. "What vote?"

"Forget it. You ain't old enough to vote."

Narrow-eyed and angry, he demanded, "You making some kind of joke at me?"

Seth shrugged.

"You don't make fun of me. You hear me, Seth!"

He studied the boy, wondering if *he'd* looked like that when he was pushing at sixteen and trying hard to be a man. If he had, it might account for more than a few of the fights he'd ended up in. He said quietly, "You know, you ain't answered me yet. They call you Chuck or Charlie?"

"Why?"

"We seem to be on first-name terms."

"You ain't got but a first name!"

Dammit, this ornery brat needed somebody to string him down a couple of pegs. He fought back the personal devil that urged him to do the job. For a long moment he and the boy just stared at each other. Then, still keeping his voice soft, he asked, "Where'd you hear that?"

"Everybody says it."

"Everybody who?"

23

Instead of answering, the kid snapped, "Why did you come back here?"

"Why not? It's my home, ain't it?"

"Like hell it is! You're *not* a Yarborough!"

The cigarette was smoldering down between Seth's fingers. He took a long drag at it. Catching his breath again, holding steady, he said, "All right, supposing I got no claim to the name of Yarborough, I was still raised here. Close to nineteen years I lived here. Why shouldn't I come back?"

"Because Pa said you shouldn't. He said for you to get and stay away!"

"Where'd you hear that? From him?"

"No, but around. Everybody says it."

"Everybody sure talks a lot."

"He *did* run you off, didn't he?"

There was no point in denying it. Seth nodded.

"Why did you come back?"

"Don't you mean why'd he let me stay?" He managed to say it with a calmness that seemed to upset the kid. Why the hell was this brat trying so hard to rankle him, he wondered. Glancing down, he saw the boy's fingers brush lightly—nervously—at the butt of the Colt revolver on his hip. Was the damn fool kid trying to provoke himself a gunfight, he thought incredulously.

They were staring silently at each other again, and Seth didn't like it at all. He didn't want trouble with anybody, especially not J.B.'s stepson. And especially not gun trouble.

The boy glanced away, then squared his shoulders. With a viciousness that was obviously intentional, he snapped out, "Did you really kill your own brother?"

If he wanted a fight he was damned sure close to getting it. Seth snubbed out the cigarette against the fence rail, ramming it down, twisting it hard. His hand quivered with tension. But he was still able to keep his voice level. "You seem to know all about everything, Chuck. Maybe you already know that Jeremy and me didn't have the same mother?"

The kid nodded, his eyes more suspicious than ever.

"Then if I'm not really J.B.'s son, Jeremy and me weren't really brothers at all, were we?"

He couldn't argue that. He stood there, looking stymied,

24

working his thumb along the butt of the Colt. Defensively, he demanded, "You *did* kill him!"

"Yeah."

"Why did you come back?" He was almost shouting now. "Do you think you can kill me, too?"

Seth stared at him, astonished. What the hell was this calf thinking? Just how wild had the gossip got in six years? Sincerely, he asked, "What kind of game do you think you're playing?"

His voice thin, but intense with challenge, the kid said, "You can't take me in a *fair* fight!"

"I ain't planning to try," Seth muttered. He didn't feel so angry now, just confused. As he slid down off the fence he saw the boy's arm jerk. Primed and cocked and hair-sprung, he thought. And crazy.

He asked, "What gives you the notion I'm looking for a fight with you?"

"Why else would you come back here?"

Sighing, he glanced at the dun inside the corral. "To grain my horse. Soon as he's rested, I'll be pulling out."

For an instant the boy seemed puzzled again. Then he decided he had the upper hand. Curling his lip, he snarled, "You're leaving *now!*"

It might have been funny—but it wasn't. Not at all. It was pure, raw trouble trying to break the thin hold he had on his own temper. Turning his back, Seth started toward the bunkhouse.

"Now!" the kid hollered, his voice almost a screech. Seth stopped. Slowly he looked over his shoulder.

Charles O'Connor Yarborough had stepped back and stood poised, crouching slightly, with his arm as stiff as a rail. His hand hovered near the ivory-butted Colt, thumb and forefinger outstretched and trembling with tension. His face was drained of color.

He looked like the drawing on the cover of a dime novel, Seth thought. He wondered if this whole business could have got its start in some illustrated weekly. Keeping his voice casual, he said, "You want to back me down? All right, I'm backed. Go brag it around the bunkhouse, if that's what you want."

He turned then, and began walking again. But he could feel an itching between his shoulder blades, as if the kid's eyes were burning into his back.

"*Face me, you bastard!*"

He stopped, catching at his breath, fighting the devil of anger that almost overwhelmed him. Was this damned bull-calf going to keep hooking at him the whole time he was stuck here? He had to find some way to put an end to this. He wasn't sure how much of it he could take before his nerves wore raw and he did some damn fool thing he'd regret forever.

"What the hell is it you want from me?"

"To settle this now!" the boy answered.

Holding his hands well away from his sides, Seth turned to face him. "Settle what?"

"I know you came here to kill me. Only you're not going to get the chance to shoot *me* in the back!"

There was fire in Seth's blood. It was a pain that scorched to his fingertips. This kid seemed to know every raw sore on his soul, and to be intent on roweling them all. A damned devil's game . . . but looking into the boy's face, he knew it was no game for Charles O'Connor Yarborough. The boy was really serious, and plenty scared. He really believed he'd been marked, and he meant to stand up and make a man's fight of it.

Maybe he wasn't a man yet, Seth thought. But for a damn fool kid, he had guts. "Why?" he asked. "What reason do you think I'd have for . . .?"

"Charles!"

It was a woman's voice, piercing and frightened. At the sound of it, the kid half wheeled, grabbing at his gun. He managed to stop his hand before he'd cleared leather. A mixture of shame and anger blazed across his face as he looked toward the woman who'd rushed out onto the gallery.

Seth was slower in turning. He'd seen the boy's move. Damned tight-strung. He felt an intense relief at this interruption.

Critically, he studied the woman. She fit Mace's description of the new Mrs. Yarborough all right. In her late thirties, though from this distance she could have passed for younger than that. Slender, tight-cinched and well-shaped. Well-dressed, too, with her pale-yellow hair caught up in a fancy sweep of curls, and lace ruffles at her sleeves and throat.

Even from where he stood, Seth could see the fire in the glance she gave him. But her attention went quickly back to the boy.

26

"Charles!" She snapped the order like a whip. "Come here this instant! Get into the house!"

The boy shot Seth a look then that was pure hatred, all of his fear overwhelmed by embarrassment. And Seth could feel a sympathy for him. The poor kid had tried making his stand as a man and right in the middle his Ma had called him to come home from play. Hell of a thing to have happen to you.

He watched Charles O'Connor Yarborough plod toward the house in humiliation. Rough for the kid, but still a damn sight better than having that hand played out to the end, he thought as he started to turn back to the bunkhouse. He felt thankful as hell that it was all over.

"You!" the woman shouted at him. "I want to talk to you!"

Chapter 3

So it *wasn't* over, Seth thought darkly. Now there'd be another damned ugly scene, this time with the boy's mother.

As he looked toward her, she repeated, "I want to talk to you. Come here."·

It should have been easy enough to walk over to the gallery and stand still for whatever kind of word-whipping she wanted to put onto him. What the hell would it matter? But the devil in him balked. Iron-mouthed, it overcame his attempt to hold it back. He'd been rawhided enough already. This woman—this new Mrs. Yarborough —had no command over him.

Jamming his hands into his pockets, he called back, "Are you paying me a wage?"

That startled her.

As if she'd given him an answer, he said, "Then go give your orders to somebody you're paying to take them."

She seemed struck speechless.

He turned and strode toward Mace's room, feeling a vague satisfaction. To hell with her. But as he shoved open the door, he heard her footsteps on the gallery stairs, tiny heels slapping the planks hard and fast.

He slammed the door shut behind him. For a moment, he stood listening. He could hear her hurrying across the packed earth of the yard. Dammit, why hadn't he stayed in Kansas and let himself be lynched in peace? He flung his hat onto the table, grabbed the scarf from around his neck, and began fingering open the buttons of his shirt. He hoped she was a proper, respectable, church-going good woman.

He was tugging off the shirt as she jerked open the door. From the corner of his eye, he saw her pause there, with the sky bright behind her. He couldn't make out the expression on her face. Pure, horrified shock, he hoped.

28

He tossed down the shirt and peeled his gunbelt. Seating himself on the edge of the bed, he began casually pulling off his boots.

She didn't move.

Without looking up, he said, "Come on in and close the door behind you."

She did.

He realized then that he'd been backed down. He'd stripped to his britches—as far as he intended to—and further than he'd expected her to stand for. Any proper lady should have stalked off, shocked and insulted. But she was just standing there, apparently unabashed by the amount of skin he'd bared. He wondered just what J.B. had got himself for a wife this time.

Looking up, he grunted, "All right."

She was slender and slightly built, but there was strength enough in her face. Cunning, too. She wasn't as casual about this as she pretended. She'd just plain called his bluff.

"So you're the notorious Seth Yarborough?"

She had a voice as sweet as fresh honey laced with coal oil. But at least she wasn't screaming at him. That was better than he'd hoped for. He nodded in reply.

"Why have you come back here?" She sounded as if she really wanted to know.

"Didn't J.B. tell you?"

"No. But I can guess."

"Then maybe you'll tell me. I'm getting real curious."

"I don't doubt that you heard about our marriage," she said. "You realized that you are no longer J.B.'s only legal heir, so you've come to see if you can work your way into his good graces again."

That surprised him in more ways than one. Surely J.B.'s fancy lawyers could have come up with an iron-bound will by now—one that would lock him completely out of inheriting any part of J.B.'s holdings without outright admitting he wasn't a Yarborough. . . .

"That's the damned funniest thing I've heard in years," he said.

"You don't stand a chance." She shook her head slowly, emphatically. "I have a great deal of influence with my husband. . . ."

"I'll just bet you have." He let his gaze move over her, with as much insult in his face as he could muster. The

29

hard set of her expression didn't change, but he could see color tinge her cheeks. Well, she could blush. She was sure fighting it though.

"He'll listen to me," she insisted, "when I tell him what you tried to do to Charles."

"Tell *me* what I tried to do to Charles. I'm right curious about that too."

She swallowed back whatever insult she'd started to throw at him. Instead, she hesitated, scanning the room thoughtfully. Likely planning a different line of attack, he figured.

"You'll only lose if you persist in this," she said quietly. "You won't get *anything* this way. But if you were to co-operate—to leave here now—I might arrange something—some expense money."

What the hell did she think he was—an animal to be bought or sold? She was a match for J.B., wasn't she? Figuring anything could be had at a price. And what did she think he was worth?

He asked, "How much?"

She studied him critically. "A thousand dollars."

Well, that was more than J.B. had paid to be rid of him. Lot more than a hundred dollars and a horse. Keeping his face expressionless, he said, "You really reckon you could buy me off that cheap?"

She glanced significantly at the battered Stetson on the table, the shirt he'd flung over a bedpost, and the Levi's worn thin where they stretched over his knees.

She nodded smugly.

Damn her! But she was right about one thing—he sure as hell wouldn't be leaving here with a cent more than he'd come with. He looked her over again, wondering how he could stab through that cool self-control and really hurt her.

"Ain't I seen you before somewhere?" he said lazily. "Maybe in New Orleans?"

Puzzled, she shook her head. "I've never been there."

He shrugged and leaned back against the headboard. "Maybe it was just somebody *like* you. Some of the fancy women down there get themselves a right good price. Nothing to compare with what you've got from J.B. though."

That sparked anger in her eyes. And this time, she couldn't hold back the rush of color to her cheeks.

There was an ugly pleasure in having cut deep. Eying her, he swung his legs up onto the bed and stretched out. "What's your price to me?" he drawled.

"What was your mother's usual charge?" she snapped back.

He felt a muscle jerk violently in his jaw. He had to force open the hand that had begun to clench itself into a fist. He hoped to hell she hadn't seen that—hoped she couldn't read in his face how deep she'd struck. It was the first time he could recall ever wanting so damned desperately to slam his fist into a woman's face.

With effort, he made himself grin at her. He had a feeling it wasn't very successful. "So J.B. wants that youngun of yours for an heir? Couldn't you do better for the old man than that? You got a father picked for the next one or . . ."

She wheeled away from his words. Her hand clawed at the knob, wrenching open the door. Her heels hit hard at the ground as she strode out.

". . . are you taking what you can get?" he finished dully. The way she'd reacted—he wondered if there really had been an O'Connor. For a long moment he didn't move. There'd been a flash of satisfaction in fighting back, really hurting her, but now it was gone. He gazed unseeing at the sky beyond the still-open door. Then slowly, jerky with tension, he got to his feet.

He picked up one of the boots he'd shucked off. Raising it overhead, he slammed it onto the floor with all his strength. The thick planks dulled its thud. And the meager violence relieved nothing.

He picked the boot up again, this time aiming it toward the glass of the window. But he stopped his hand. Damned little good it would do—just give *her* the satisfaction of knowing how deep she'd managed to hurt him.

Seating himself on the edge of the bed, he began to pull the boots on again. When he tugged the shirt over his shoulders the stale feel of it didn't bother him. His skin no longer felt clean.

Dressed, he leaned against the door jamb and gazed at the back of the big house. It loomed, overpowering the whole of the ranch. Hell of a place. So she wanted the Yarborough holdings for herself. Well, as far as he was concerned, she could have them. He was sick of the sight of the place. Sick of the whole damned JayBar. He

31

wouldn't have a handspan of the Yarborough land if they gold-plated it.

He headed for the corral and grabbed down a throw rope from a post. The dun needed rest, but there were other good horses behind the rails. That long-legged bay geld looked like an animal that could stretch out and go. Blooded horse, from the build of it. But then J.B. wouldn't have anything except the best money could buy, would he?

The bay didn't fight the rope. He threw his saddle on its back and jerked up the cinches sharply. Gigging the horse as he swung on board, he reined toward the slopes of Bloodyhead Mountain.

As soon as the horse had limbered, he spurred it into a run. At first he'd been sorry it hadn't shown him any fight under the saddle. But as it stepped out now, he decided he'd made a good choice. This bay was little brother to the wind, smooth-striding and sure-footed. There was a clean, honest pleasure in forking a good horse, riding hard and riding well.

He ran out of open country and had to ease the pace as he headed into the forest. But he kept the horse moving fast along the game trail he'd chosen. As he bent low in the saddle, branches whipped close over his head and stung his shoulders. Like the old man's strap, he thought, only with the trees it wasn't intentional. They didn't mean to hurt him.

The stretch of woods ended abruptly at a steep, rocky slope. He drove the horse down recklessly, feeling it slide on its haunches, grabbing for footholds. Reaching level ground again, he spurred it into another hard run. He held it to the pace until he could no longer ignore the signs of its tiring.

There was no sense in driving a good horse to death, he told himself, even if it was one of J.B.'s horses. The animal couldn't be held to blame for that. Probably had the damned bad luck to be born on JayBar land.

He eased to a lope, then drew rein to let the horse blow. Sighing, catching breath himself, he discovered he'd almost managed to outrun his devil. The anger was about gone. What he felt now was just a hollow weariness.

He sat a while, waiting as the heaving of the horse's ribs eased and its breathing grew even again. Then he ambled it on through the next patch of woods, and up to the crest of a rock-strewn ridge. From there he could look out at the broad basin of a valley.

The patches of open meadow below shone brilliant green, and the stands of pine rose straight as arrows. Across the valley a wall of ridges lay dappled by shadows of huge white clouds. The misty blue mountains were marked with while flecks that were hollows holding snow cupped in them all through the year.

It had been a hell of a long time since he'd seen these mountains. He gazed thoughtfully at the outcrops of bare gray rock, the blue-green spruce, and the long rolling bottomland of lush graze. Good country, worth traveling a way to look at. Country that made a man feel hungry for the sight of it.

Swinging the bay down the back of the ridge, then across, he turned onto a slope covered with forest. The game trail twisted, climbed, dropped, and then broke abruptly into a meadow high on the side of Bloodyhead. It was a broad green sweep of wild grass better than hock-deep, flecked with moonpennies and blowballs and sparkling in the sunlight.

He took a deep breath of its fresh scents, then stepped down and stripped his gear off the horse. It nosed eagerly into the grass, nibbling over his shoulder as he hunkered to put the hobbles on it. Then he walked out toward the middle of the field and stretched himself on the ground.

He lay there, feeling the sunlight warm against his face, seeing it bright against his closed eyelids. It seeped into his muscles and he could feel it working away the tightness. Lazily, he turned to let it beat down on his back. He rested his head on his arm, his eyes still closed. It was good to lie here with the smell of the meadow grass as sweet as honey so close to his face.

As far as he was concerned, they could have the whole of Texas, with Kansas and the territories thrown in, for one square mile of Bloodyhead's slopes.

Funny how J.B. had always talked so highly of Texas. But then the devil was probably proud of Hell, too. Oh sure, there were parts of Texas that weren't so bad, but the brasada, the llano, the vast flat miles of nothing—that was the land J.B. had been raised in and had bragged on and had fought the Mexicans for back in the '30's. But despite all his talk, the old man had packed up and come here, hadn't he? He'd driven his stakes here in the mountains of Colorado.

Seth remembered the stories the way he'd heard them, the way he'd pieced them together from talk.

J.B.'d had a spread of some kind down there in Texas a long time back. But he'd lost it to Comanche raiders. Lost everything he'd had. He'd managed to make it into the nearest town with nothing but one horse and a pregnant wife. And she had died a few days later giving birth to the first boy, Jeremy.

Then the old man went to hunt himself up a second wife the same way a person might hunt a fresh cow to nurse an orphaned calf. He'd bought himself a woman to stepmother Jeremy. And to bear Seth.

Not long after the marriage, J.B.'d scraped together an outfit and moved his family up into Jeff Territory, along with a wagonload of trade goods. What kind, Seth wondered, whiskey and guns?

The Yarboroughs had settled here when the second boy was born. J.B.'s foothold had been secure even before the silver strikes were made in these mountains and a town suddenly grew up around the springs on the old trail.

When the high-grade ore petered out and the boom town of Jubilee began to die as fast as it had grown, J.B.'d stayed on and acquired land from the men who moved out. The War of the Rebellion had been going on in the States then, and he was turning himself a good profit from it, making long trips to unnamed places.

It was after the war that Jubilee started to grow again. The new mining and milling methods made it profitable to reopen some of the old diggings. J.B. was one of the men who supplied financing. And he backed the building of the railroad through Jubilee.

He'd been the first to bring cattle into Long County on a grand scale, too. He'd been a cattleman in Texas and when he looked at these green parks and slopes, he saw them as graze. So he'd brought in beef animals. Then other men began to do the same. And it was J.B. who organized the Association. It was J.B. who presided over it.

Sure, the JayBar was no longer the biggest single spread around here now. Sure, there was a lot of land J.B. didn't have title to, a lot of property he didn't hold mortgages on and businesses he didn't have interests in. But still he owned Long County. He owned it with power and influence. That was what really counted to the old man, Seth thought. Being King of the Hill. Owning influence, owning money, owning people as if they were so many head of cattle to be marked with the JayBar brand and driven where he pleased to drive them. . . .

With a start Seth came awake. There was a horse coming toward him—real close—almost on top of him. He jumped up.

The horse reared, throwing its shadow across him. A sorrel mare, rising up on its hind legs, pawing frantically at the sky. Nostrils flared, it stared white-eyed at him, bad scared by the way he'd suddenly risen out of the deep grass.

The girl on its back grabbed rein, looking scared herself. He glimpsed her face, saw her skirts billow as the sorrel wheeled to bolt.

Lunging, he caught at the bridle. His fingers clamped over the reins close to the bit. The horse tossed its upraised head, trying to pull free of him. But he clung, fighting it with his full weight. And slowly it came down.

With its forehooves on the ground again, the horse began to settle. He turned his attention to the girl on its back then. She looked dazed, pale and uncertain.

"You all right?" he asked.

She nodded. In a small, shaky voice, she said, "Help me down, please."

He held out a hand to her, steadying her as she stepped from the sidesaddle. He could feel her fear in the trembling of her hand. She didn't seem hurt, but she'd been badly startled.

"Sorry," he said. "I didn't mean to spook your horse that way. Are you sure you're all right?"

She caught her breath. Pulling her hand away from his, she brushed at a strand of hair that had fallen loose over her forehead. It was yellow hair, fine and light, softly framing her face. It was a nice face, he thought. A real attractive face.

The color was coming back to her cheeks. With a small smile, she said, "I should pay more attention to where I'm going. But I saw your horse there and I was curious about him." She shrugged toward the hobbled bay. "You're new at JayBar, aren't you?"

"What makes you think I'm from JayBar?"

"I know the Yarborough brand."

"A man doesn't always work for the brand he rides."

Her eyes were blue—a bright, bold blue that came close to being violet-tinged. They held to his, looking as if there were laughter just behind them. He admired the way she filled out the dark-blue riding suit she wore. About nineteen, he judged, sound of wind and limb. . . .

And she was over her scare now. With that hint of a smile still on her lips, she answered, "I know that horse. He's one of Mister Yarborough's prize string and not for sale. And you don't look like a horse thief."

It was pleasant to talk to her. He asked, "You know many horse thieves?"

She shook her head.

"Then what makes you so sure I'm not one?"

Pursing her lips, she pretended to study him critically. "You just don't—oh—you're Seth! Seth Yarborough!"

With a delighted laugh, she threw her arms around his neck.

He didn't know who she might be. For the moment, it didn't seem to matter. He held her, bending his face toward hers. But then she was pulling out of his arms.

He made no attempt to stop her.

For an instant, she faced him silently. But then she laughed again, as if she hadn't felt his hands or understood how close his mouth had been. Forcing a mock scowl, she said, "You don't remember me, do you?"

He didn't like being called to admit he didn't know something. But this time, he wasn't angry. Reluctantly, he shook his head. Try as he might, he couldn't put a name to that lovely face.

"I'm Annie Johnson."

He stepped back and took a good look at her, amazed by what six years could do for a bratty little girl. Then he grinned. "You've grown, Annie Johnson."

She brushed at her skirt and posed for him. "Glad?"

"Real glad. You've sure changed."

"You've changed too, Seth."

Was that an accusation? He glanced at his clothes, thinking that the last time she'd seen him, he'd looked a damn sight better than this. The moment of silence felt awkward. He groped for something bright to say—something pointless that would distract her—something she could smile at again. But he found nothing.

36

"Sure, we all change," he heard himself mumble. That seemed like a damned stupid thing to say.

He thought he saw disappointment in her eyes. She reached out for the reins he held, her fingers brushing his as she took them. Gathering her skirts, she said, "Give me a hand up, Seth."

"Don't go yet!"

She looked at him questioningly.

"I just got back last night," he said. "Stay here a while and catch me up on the news. What's been happening around here since I left?"

"Nothing. Nothing ever happens around here. I'd rather hear what you've been doing. Where have you been?"

"Out looking at the rest of the world."

"How does it look?" Her eyes were bold, teasing.

"Not nearly as good as you do." He held a hand out to her. "Come sit with me and tell me about yourself, Annie.

But she turned away from him. He glimpsed the flush of color that came to her face and he cursed himself silently for being so damned forward with her. She might have bold eyes, but she was no saloon girl. And he was certain she knew how close he'd been to kissing her. He figured he deserved at least a slap in the face for that. It was no way to act with a girl like Annie, even if they had both been kids on the same range.

He wondered what she was thinking of him now. Likely the worst. Dammit, he knew better than to act that way, didn't he? Now she woudln't know what to expect from him. Hell, he wasn't too sure what to expect from himself.

He jammed his hands into his pockets and gazed at the ground, feeling cheap and shamed. But he didn't want her to leave. Maybe he could make her understand. Hopefully, he suggested, "Maybe we could ride a ways together? Maybe—look, I promise I'll behave."

Her mouth hinted a smile as she looked at him again with those teasing blue eyes. They gave him the uncomfortable feeling that she knew secrets about him. Fighting back the smile, she said, "Swear me a solemn and horrible oath on that, Seth Yarborough."

He felt a sharp relief. If she could joke about it, she wasn't mad at him. Raising his right hand, he tried to match her mock seriousness. "I swear a solemn and horrible oath I'll behave."

37

"On your honor as a gentleman."

"Won't be binding if I add that." He grinned as he picked up his saddle. He slung it onto the bay and cinched up quickly.

They ride together at a slow amble, talking about a lot of things—nothing in particular—old and trivial memories—keeping it to that. He felt as if he'd never known her well. When he was a kid she had been just a baby. And when she'd reached kid-size, he'd considered himself a grown man and above noticing a freckle-faced brat, especially one that had been as much of a plaguey pest as Annie Johnson had been. He recalled her mostly for the way she'd had of suddenly showing up on the range, during roundup, or in town, butting into things and getting in the way. A damn nuisance, he had thought at the time. It had seemed to him then as if she had singled him out to pester on purpose.

She remembered a lot about him, though. He was amazed by how much she recalled—even to things like the way he'd creased his hat and knotted his bandanna then. She reminded him of parties he'd forgotten and could even tell him what girl he'd been squiring to each of them.

They were laughing together when they caught sight of a thin twist of smoke curling up from a chimney over the rise. That was the Johnson place, he realized with a strong sense of disappointment.

Annie stopped her horse, and he halted beside her. So this was as far as he could ride with her. He said, "I don't reckon your folks would approve much of me."

"They wouldn't approve much of my riding alone with *any* young man they hadn't met properly first. If they knew, they might even object to my riding back that way tomorrow."

"Tomorrow?"

She nodded. Turning her horse away from him, she looked back over her shoulder. "That same park. I ride up that way a lot. If you were to happen to be there tomorrow about the same time, we just might run into each other again."

He sat there, watching her and knowing there was a damn silly grin on his face. He watched until she had topped the ridge and disappeared beyond it. Then he wheeled the bay, setting it into a run, riding fast and hard for the joy of it.

He didn't want to go back to JayBar. Not now. This world was too fine for him to give it up and go back into that little hell. He swung the bay in a wide loop.

It was getting late, he realized, and he was getting hungry. The town of Jubilee wasn't a far ride from the Johnson place. He considered, deciding he still had coin enough in his poke to indulge himself in a bought meal. And maybe a couple of drinks. He felt like celebrating.

Chapter 4

It wasn't until he was within sight of the town that Seth recalled what Mace had told him: J.B.'d said that he should stay on JayBar land. To hell with that. J.B. could go whistle.

He reined onto the main street, feeling a perverse pleasure in bucking the old man's orders again. J.B. was supposed to be in town now himself, he thought as he scanned the people on the walks. What was the chance of their running into each other? Well, if that happened and the old man started raising hell, he'd get it right back.

He picked out a few faces that he could still put names to, and more that were vaguely familiar. But no one seemed to pay him any particular attention. Not as he rode in, or as he sat eating in a scrubby little café near the railroad depot. That was just fine. He really didn't want to run into anyone he'd known. Didn't want to have to make talk or explain himself. More likely, though, there wouldn't be any talk—not to his face. Just stares and whispers behind his back.

It was getting dark when he left the café. He strode across Long Street toward the Grand Palace Saloon. Only its front lamps were lit, and it was pretty quiet-looking inside. Usually was on a weekday like this. He ambled in and leaned on the bar, giving his order to the bartender without showing any sign of recognition.

He remembered the saloon keeper well enough though. Tucker had always been a decent sort, even if he had raised hell every time the boys started a ruckus in his place, and had always overcharged J.B. for any damage that was done.

As he picked up his drink, he looked at his image in the backbar mirror. No reason to be surprised that Tucker didn't remember him, he decided. Recalling the reflection that had looked back at him the last time he'd stood here, he wondered how much of the difference was just clothes, and how much in his face itself. Been a hell of a lot younger face then, fleshier and softer, even if it had already begun to show that same narrowed set to the eyes and mouth.

He savored the whiskey, thinking it was a damn sight better stuff than drovers got shoved off on them in trail towns like Horseshoe. As he swallowed the last of it, one of the reflections in the mirror caught his eye. The man looked away quick as Seth glanced at his image. But Seth was certain he'd been staring at him.

The man was across the room. He walked up to the bar and called for a drink. Furtively, he looked into the mirror again—at Seth again. The third time, their eyes met in the silvering and held for an instant.

Wheeling to face the man instead of the reflection, Seth demanded, "Something about me you don't like, Mister?"

He judged this man to be about a year older than himself, a couple of inches taller and quite a few pounds heavier. His hands looked competent. The scars were from grass rope, but the knuckles seemed hard and capable. These were the things Seth judged first. Then he cast about for a name to put to the vaguely familiar face.

"You're Seth Yarborough, ain't you?" the man said.

Seth nodded slowly. He'd found the name. This was Bud Tatum. He remembered Bud damned well—with rising hatred.

It had been a long time ago, not much after his mother had died, that J.B. first sent him in to school with Jeremy. Mister Hawkes had taught with a sharp-pointed finger and a hickory ruler and had quickly convinced most of his pupils that they didn't really want book-learning, but were stuck with it anyway. One of those pupils had been Bud Tatum.

Seth remembered the day. It had been a damned miserable one to begin with. His mother's death had left him with a lost and lonely feeling. He hadn't wanted anything to do with the other kids anyway. But they'd cornered him not far from the school and set in to teaching him a new word—bastard.

They had explained it to him with detail that had ended in a fight. A damned one-sided fight with Seth pinned, flailing, screaming, crying, while Bud Tatum straddled his

41

chest and hammered at him. The others had surrounded them, urging Bud on.

Finally, after what had seemed like an eternity, Jeremy had answered his screams. Jeremy, who was two years older than Seth, and Yarborough-big, had come and broken it up. He'd chased off Tatum and the others. But when he'd offered Seth his hand, Seth had lit into him.

Seth remembered that day. He counted it as the start of a long education. That was when he'd first begun to learn that if he cried when he was hit, he got hit again. So he learned not to cry. He discovered that if other people knew the things he cared about—the things that really mattered to him—they could turn on him and hurt him. So he began to learn not to show that he cared. And he learned ways to hit back—to hurt them in return.

The memory starkly vivid now, he looked into the face of Bud Tatum. His right hand had unwrapped itself from the empty glass and dropped to his side, open and ready. He hadn't given thought to anything like this when he decided to ride into town. He hadn't thought at all about the old hatreds, hadn't realized how easily they might be stirred into fresh fire. But now they burned as hot as they had six and more years ago.

Grinning sociably, as if he understood nothing of this, Tatum said, "You recollect me, don't you, Seth? I'm Bud Tatum."

"I recall you." Seth's voice was like the cold buzz of a snake's buttons.

"Can I buy you a drink?" Tatum offered.

"Why?"

He looked puzzled by Seth's tone. The grin weakened, almost sliding off his face.

What the hell did he expect, Seth thought. To be greeted like some long-lost friend? Didn't *he* remember?

Sounding tentative, almost apologetic, Tatum said, "I never got a chance to tell you before—I was real sorry about Jeremy. He was a fine feller."

Tensely, Seth gazed at him. What reason could Tatum have for mentioning Jeremy—except as an indirect accusation of murder?

The bartender had come back toward them, close enough to catch a few words. He interrupted with a broad grin. "Migod, Seth Yarborough! I thought I knew you from somewheres, only I couldn't quite place you."

42

Seth gave him a quick glance. So they were crowding him now—ganging up on him and closing in. Well, if that was how they meant to play it, they'd find out it took more than a couple of dumb sons like them to outnumber Seth Yarborough. He didn't need a big brother to rescue him any more. He could take care of himself now.

"Good to see you again," Tucker was saying. "You've sure changed."

As he started to snap back at the man's sarcasm, Seth looked into his face. He caught himself before he spoke. Tucker looked *sincere*. Frowning, he echoed the man's words in his mind, listening for that sarcasm he'd thought he heard in them. He turned to Bud Tatum, searching for some trace of hostility in his eyes. He didn't find it.

"This round's on the house," Tucker said heartily as he refilled their glasses and set one up for himself. He held it out, "Welcome home, Seth. Good to see you again."

"Yeah—sure," Seth mumbled, bewildered now himself. Was it possible that these two fools really meant what they were saying? He asked Tatum, "Don't you recall? We fought each other like a couple of studs. We hated each other's guts."

The man grinned, "I sure do remember. For a kid your size, you sure belted hell out of me a couple of times."

"Wild young'uns," Tucker agreed. "And you were the wildest of the lot, Seth."

Kids, Seth thought dully. Was that all it had been to them—kid stuff? Did they have any idea how close his hand had been to his gun just now?

Gazing at Tatum's face, he had a sudden feeling that this wasn't the same person at all—not the kid he'd hated so intensely for so many years. Tatum probably didn't even recall now why they'd fought each other in those days. And you don't jump a man for something he doesn't remember.

The anger was gone. Dead and cold. Seth felt shaken— aware now of how close he'd just come to serious trouble —maybe gun trouble. It was as though he'd stepped back six years and had been a feisty kid again with his temper as tight-wound and hair-triggered as it had ever been. Why? Because of something he'd *imagined*?

He reached for the drink. He felt the need of it.

Whatever Tatum was saying wasn't important. Just friendly conversation. Seth only mumbled back in response to the tone of his voice. But Tatum seemed satisfied. He nodded and asked, "You been up to the ranch yet?"

Seth grunted again, wondering if he was getting at something in particular.

"Wait'll you see the house J.B.'s built up there," Tatum said enthusiastically.

Seth had to stop himself short again. He'd almost snapped out a vicious reply. He was sure now that this poor dolt wasn't prodding him on purpose. But it was hard as hell to keep from finding sharp points in his words and jabbing back at them.

He felt damned uncomfortable, embarrassed at how close he'd come to letting the devil in him take the reins, and afraid that it still might happen. As quickly as he could without seeming to rush, he finished off the drink. Touching his hat brim to the two of them, he left.

The wonderfully pleasant feeling he'd had when he parted with Annie Johnson was completely gone now. The drinks only seemed to have made him sleepy. He felt confused, but too washed out and weary to try straightening his thoughts. Settling into the saddle, he turned his horse uproad toward JayBar. It was a fair long ride.

The horse was tired too. He could feel it. But the animal knew it was heading back to the ranch and feed now, and it held a steady pace. Seth let himself doze in the saddle.

It was hard to rouse himself from the fuzzy uncertain dreams as he neared the house. He stretched his shoulders and rubbed at his eyes. Reining onto the driveway, he looked up at the mansion. Its dark bulk loomed against the star-washed sky. The reflection of the almost full moon caught in one of the big glass windows upstairs. It looked like the moon was trapped there, inside that house. Alone and cold, it gazed desperately through the panes of glass, dreaming of escape.

J.B. would like that, Seth thought. The old man would be real happy to catch the moon and lock it up in there. He glanced over his shoulder at the real moon, wild and free in the sky. Some folk said it looked like a silver dollar, but it didn't. Not at all. And money wouldn't buy it either. How tall a stack of silver dollars would it take to reach from here to the moon? Likely even J.B. didn't have that much money.

As he came into the back yard, he drew rein sharply, suddenly aware that he wasn't alone. Maybe it was a scent

44

or sound too soft for him to know he'd heard it, but he had a strong feeling there was another person here, right close by. He scanned the yard and the shadows of the outbuildings. Then he looked at the back gallery of the big house. He spotted the dark blur against the pale lines of the whitewashed railing. It looked like an old bundle left propped on the top step.

He touched spurs lightly to the horse's flanks, ambling it toward the steps. As he stopped, he grinned to himself. It was the kid, Charles O'Connor Yarborough, sitting there sound asleep with his head lobbed against the rails. Damn fool kid ought to be in bed at this hour.

He leaned on the saddle fork and called softly, "Hey, Hardcase."

The boy stirred a bit. But Seth had to call again before he lifted his head and blinked open his eyes.

"Huh?" he grunted dully.

"If you're waiting for Santa Claus, you're too early," Seth said.

"Waitin' for *you*," the kid mumbled, his voice sullen and sleepy.

Seth felt fuzzy with the dregs of sleep himself. He had a vague notion that he shouldn't be amused by the kid. But right now he was. He said, "You ain't planning to start any gunplay at this hour, are you, Chuck? Don't want to wake your Ma. She needs her beauty sleep."

The boy yawned and rubbed his face. He seemed to be having a hard time bringing himself around. Stiffly, he got to his feet and faced Seth.

"You leave my Ma alone," he tried to sound hard, but he almost yawned again in the middle of his words.

Seth was still grinning to himself. "Young'un like you ought to have been tucked in hours ago."

"You leave my Ma alone," the boy repeated, this time with more control over his voice.

"Be glad to. Reckon you could talk her into leaving me alone, too?"

"What do you mean?"

Seth's grin was fading. Dammit, this kid was proddy, and awake enough now to start turning ugly. He was coming awake now himself, realizing there was nothing here to be amused at. Lifting rein, he swung the bay around.

"What do you mean about my Ma?" Chuck called at his back.

Ugly and noisy. Ignoring him, Seth jogged the horse toward the corral. He could hear the kid hurry down the steps and across the yard after him. Why the hell had he wakened the boy in the first place? he asked himself. Why the hell had he mocked the kid? He should have realized what he'd be starting.

As he stepped out of the saddle, Chuck came up behind him. Turning, he began, "Look here now . . ."

The kid swung. He tried for Seth's face. Seth saw the fist and caught the blow easily enough, blocking it with his arm. He didn't want to hit this boy. But he couldn't stop him. Arms flailing, head ducked, Chuck tried to close.

It was no contest. The kid was all fury but without skill. Seth held him off for a moment. Then with a grunt of disgust, he landed a fist under the boy's breastbone. Stunned, Chuck sprawled back against the corral rails. He slid to the ground and lay there, gasping for breath.

Seth turned toward the bunkhouse. Its windows had sprung alive with lamplight. Dark shadows cut across the glow and the door swung open. Half-dressed men were rushing toward him, moving to circle him.

His fingers brushed the butt of the Colt he wore. Glancing from the men to the still form of the boy and back again, he jerked his hand away from the gun. So he'd punched Charles O'Connor Yarborough. The damn fool kid had forced him to it. Waving a gun now would just make things look worse.

He stood, tight-strung and sure there'd be trouble. There always was. He'd made a mistake and it had built on itself. He didn't want to add to it. He fought back the urge to pull his gun and get himself the hell away from the cowhands who were surrounding him.

"What's happened?" someone shouted.

"Nothing," he snapped back. They didn't believe him, he thought. He hadn't expected them to.

They muttered among themselves. And they caught sight of the kid lying with his head propped against the bottom rail of the fence.

Suddenly there were hands reaching for Seth's arms. He jerked away as they grabbed at him. There were too many of them, too close. They gripped his arms, holding

46

him. He swallowed at the urge to shout—to lash out and fight.

One of the men hunkered at the boy's side. "It's Charles."

"Is he dead?" another asked.

"No."

"What's happened here?" someone else demanded.

Seth scanned them, these shadows in the night that held him. He couldn't see their faces, but he could feel their anger. And their hands were on him, fingers biting into his arms. He hated that. It stirred a sense of panic in his gut. Why the devil hadn't he drawn, held them back at gunpoint while he explained?

A flash of light caught his attention. He saw Mace striding toward the bunch, holding up a lantern.

Stepping up to him, lifting it in front of his face, Mace said, "Seth! What the hell's going on here?"

With a calm he didn't feel, Seth nodded toward Chuck. "The kid there tripped over something. His own feet, I reckon."

"Sounded like a fight to me," one of the cowhands offered. "I'm sure I heard the boy hollering."

Over Mace's shoulder, Seth glimpsed lamplight in one of the windows of the mansion. It moved to another, then the door opened. So they'd heard the ruckus up there too.

Mace was hunkering to look at the boy. As he held his lantern over Chuck's face, the woman screamed. She ran from the gallery, rushing across the yard with her wrapper clutched around her.

"Charles!" she called. "What's happened to Charles!"

"Nothing!" Seth snapped at her. "He's all right."

He felt the hands tighten on his arms again. What the hell did they think he was going to do, bust loose and tear the damned place apart?

As the woman reached him, Chuck stirred. Shaking his head, he groped for a fence rail and pulled himself up. He looked as if he was still plenty dazed as he braced himself and squinted at his mother.

"Charles, darling!" She was almost in tears. She held her arms out to him, meaning to hug him to her.

He pulled away, muttering, "Hell, Ma . . ."

The kid was a damn sight more embarrassed than he was hurt, Seth thought. Didn't that fool woman understand anything about how a boy felt? He decided she didn't.

47

Firming up her voice, she ordered her son. "You get back to the house this instant! You ought to be in bed . . ."

"He's all right," Seth snapped again. "He might even grow up into a man, if you'll give him the chance!"

Ignoring him, she waved a hand toward the house. "Charles!"

One of the cowhands snickered. Chuck shot an angry glance at the man. Bitterly, his head down, he started across the yard at his mother's command.

Resentment flared in Seth as if she'd thrown those orders at him. He shouted, "Give the goddamned kid a chance . . . !"

She wheeled to face him. The light of Mace's lantern reflected in her still-damp eyes as if fires burned there. With all her strength, she swung her open hand.

The slap stung Seth's face. But it hurt deeper. Suddenly, he couldn't stand the touch of the hands that pinned him. These damned cowboys had crowded in on him, outnumbering him. They'd grabbed at him, meaning to hold him helpless. And he couldn't take any more of it. He lunged.

Their attention had been turned toward Lucille Yarborough. Seth's move was quick, startling them. He jerked free of their grip. The anger in him was too much. He had to smash out, ease it in violence. Twisting, he threw the full weight of his move behind his clenched fist. He aimed for the nearest cowhand, and his hand rammed hard into the man's gut, carrying him back, slamming him into the corral fence.

They seemed frozen for an instant, these startled men who surrounded Seth. And then they moved to grab at him again.

He spun, swinging, this time with his gun weighting his hand. He felt his knuckles strike flesh and heard a gasp of pain.

"Keep your goddamned hands off me!" he shouted, taking a step back, away from them. The gun was leveled now, threatening them. He could feel the corral rails suddenly at his back. Closed in—his back to the fence—cornered—but he had a gun in his hand. And the men surrounding him saw it. They yielded, opening a space around him.

"Take it easy, Seth," Mace said, his voice soft and coaxing, as if he were talking to a spooked animal.

The anger was burning in Seth, but the sense of panic

was gone. Steady now, he said coldly, "Send this wolf-pack back to its hole."

He glanced around at the men, then looked straight at the woman and added, "Get this she-bitch away too."

He was aware of the sparks his words struck against the men surrounding him. He knew that they might have tried jumping him again for that. But the light of Mace's lantern showed them his face as well as the gun he held. And they stood motionless, muttering among themselves, hating him and afraid of him, and hating themselves for their fear.

Seth made a slight, threatening gesture with the revolver. He looked at the men. "Go on—git!"

They were afraid, but they weren't ready to break and run from him. Seth knew that a word from Mace, one way or the other, would move them. They'd leave—or they'd try jumping him. All they needed was Mace's command.

But Mace was standing motionless himself, gazing at Seth uncertainly.

"Mace," Seth said, more quietly now. "Get rid of them."

Nodding, Mace grunted, "Go on back to the bunkhouse."

The men turned away reluctantly. They whispered and glanced back, but they left. And Seth stood without speaking until they were all gone, all back inside the bunkhouse.

The woman hadn't moved. She still faced him defiantly. The gun he held didn't seem to bother her. What the hell did she want, he thought. Why couldn't she leave him alone?

He twisted up a corner of his mouth. His voice as vicious as he could make it, he said, "You run along now, Stepmother Yarborough. Or do you want me to come and tuck you in?"

"Goddammit, Seth!" Mace snapped. He started angrily, his fists clenched. But he held himself back.

Lucille stood tall, poised, but with the fire inside her flaring, making her face hard and ugly. Her lips moved, but made no sound. It was as if there weren't any words to express her feelings.

She found a way. She swung again, her hand slapping hard against Seth's face. It stung, but this time there was no pain—just the sharp satisfaction of knowing he'd hurt her.

Wheeling, she strode toward the house.

"Goddammit, Seth," Mace said again. He stood there, holding up the lantern, his own face lit by it now. He seemed caught within his own confusion.

The anger in Seth was fading, and with it that ugly sense of satisfaction. He felt tired, too weary to hold up the weight of the revolver in his hand. Slipping it back into the holster, he turned away from Mace.

He had to work at holding his hands steady as he stripped his saddle off the bay. He could feel the small muscles twitching in his shoulders now. And his hands were clammy on the leather as he dragged the saddle down.

He headed toward the shed with it and once he was inside—once he was hidden from Mace's sight—he dropped it and leaned, exhausted, against the wall. Wiping his face with his sleeve, he sighed and drew a deep breath. The cocked-spring tension in his belly was slowly easing.

How the hell had all that happened, he asked himself. It had turned damned ugly so damned fast. All he'd meant to do was wake up the kid and send him in to bed where he belonged. But then it had gotten out of hand. How the hell did things like that happen?

He had a feeling he knew the answer. It was because he'd said the wrong damned things. He always did, even when he knew beforehand that they were wrong.

He wiped his sweat-damp hands down his thighs and walked back out of the shed. But Mace was gone. Relieved at that, he busied himself with loosing the bay into the corral, watching it roll, and then putting out feed for it. Finally, when he felt he'd stalled around as long as he could, he headed toward the foreman's quarters.

He stood with one hand on the door, thinking he could go bed down in the barn instead. But Mace might read his reason and know he hadn't had nerve enough to face him again. Bedamned! If Mace wanted to give him hell about that ruckus, he'd give it right back.

Defiantly, he shoved open the door and stepped in.

The room was empty. Both puzzled and glad, Seth located his quilts in the dark and bedded himself. Mace still hadn't come in when he finally fell asleep.

Chapter 5

Seth woke while Mace was dressing. He showed no sign, but kept still, trying to look as if he was still asleep. He felt like hell about that ruckus last night. And he admitted to himself that it had been at least partly his own fault. He knew Mace would be expecting some kind of an explanation. But he couldn't make one, so he waited, hoping it wouldn't take Mace too long to get moving.

Only Mace didn't leave. He dressed slowly, sat sipping his coffee, and finally bent to shake Seth's shoulder.

There was no pretending to ignore that big, hard-gripping hand. Blinking as if he were still half-asleep, Seth mumbled, "What's the matter?"

"I got to talk to you. About that business last night . . ."

"Ask Chuck. *He* jumped *me*."

"That ain't what I mean. I'm talking about Lucille Yarborough," Mace answered sharply. "I won't hear nobody talk to her the way you did."

"What do you want me to do? Apologize?"

"Hell no! You stay away from her. Don't you say nothing to her again. Nothing at all, you hear me?"

"You giving me orders now, Mace?"

The foreman eyed him coldly. "You stay away from her. If you so much as say good morning, you make a body fighting mad. You're a damned swine. The old man won't have you under his roof. You say one more word about Lucille, and you ain't gonna be welcome under mine either!"

Dammit, this mess wasn't *all* his fault, Seth thought. He snapped, "That she-cow started up with me twice now. If she tries . . ."

"Goddamn you!" Mace shouted at him.

He saw the foreman's big hands knot into fists so tight that the knuckles stood out like bare bone. Struggling back the urge to strike first, he said, "What the hell am I supposed to do, Mace? Stand around chewing my cud like a yoke ox?"

"You don't get nothing you don't ask for. You're a damned rank sonofabitch and you always have been, long as I can remember. You open your mouth about Lucille once more and I'll bust your jaw!" Mace thundered. He looked almost sick with rage.

Seth stared at him. He'd never seen Mace like this before. It shocked him out of answering back in kind. What the hell was happening now? he asked himself.

When he made no reply, Mace eased a bit. But the anger still twisted the foreman's voice, as he demanded, "You understand?"

"Yeah."

He seemed more or less satisfied with that. He straightened up, slapping his hat on his head, and stalked out, slamming the door behind him.

Seth shrugged out of the quilts, got up and poured himself some coffee. It was lukewarm. He put it back into the pot and poked up the fire. As he waited for it to heat, he eyed his reflection in the mirror.

A damned rank sonofabitch?

What the hell had gotten Mace so proddy? The big Texan had always been the soft-spoken peacemaker around JayBar. Seth couldn't count the number of times Mace had taken him aside to tell him about ugly talk that was going around, always pleading with him not to pay it any mind. And when he and Jeremy squabbled, it was usually Mace who had butted in to tell them they were *supposed* to be brothers, why couldn't they act like it . . . it was even Mace who had suggested they pack out on that hunting trip to make up a fight that had drawn a little blood. Mace had always been the peacemaker.

Seth poured himself coffee again. This time it was too hot. It burnt his tongue. He sat down, cradling the cup in his hands, thinking about it all.

Mace just didn't understand what kind of a she-bitch this new Mrs. Yarborough was. He had to own he'd talked pretty hard to her. No way to talk to a lady. But she was damned far from being one.

Wasn't likely he could explain that to Mace, though. And he sure didn't want to end up fighting Mace. Best thing would be to stay away from the bitch, he decided.

Yeah, stay away from J.B., stay away from his wife, and stay away from her crazy son . . . but don't go off JayBar land. What the hell was he supposed to do—crawl into a hole and pull the lid shut? Or maybe he should make them all happy—give himself up and be hanged.

He sipped at the coffee, remembering the strange dream he'd had. In it, he'd been holding Chuck helpless with one hand while he smashed the other into the boy's face. Viciously, over and over again, and then suddenly it hadn't been Chuck at all, but himself he'd been beating hell out of. That had just made him madder, made him hit harder. Damned strange dream. Just thinking about it gave him an unpleasant feeling.

He sighed, trying to push the memory out of his mind, wondering what the hell he could do with himself for the rest of the morning. When he'd finished the coffee, he nudged open the door and looked out cautiously, as if he were afraid of finding someone waiting for him on the other side.

The only person within sight was a ranch hand leading a small black horse under a sidesaddle. For the new Mrs. Yarborough, he thought. Maybe she was going out for a while. It would sure ease his mind if he knew he wouldn't run into her.

He followed the hand at a distance. From the corner of the house, he watched Lucille Yarborough mount up and start away. He ducked, hurrying back to the yard ahead of the cowhand.

When the man got there, Seth was standing with his hands jammed into his pockets, idly gazing at the horses in the corral. Catching a horse for himself, the cowhand saddled up and rode off. Once he was gone from sight, Seth turned toward the big house.

It didn't look so damned foreboding now that he knew both J.B. and that woman were gone out of it for a while. A vague curiosity about the inside of the mansion began to stir in him. Not quite sure what he meant to do, he walked over and up onto the back gallery.

He contemplated the door. Then, careful not to let it squeak on its hinges, he edged it open. Stepping inside, he found himself in a hallway with more doors leading

53

off from it. The one to his right was open, so he glanced in.

This was the kitchen, a big room four steps down to its stone floor. It was filled with the warm, overwhelming aroma of baking bread. He took a deep breath, reminded now of how long it had been since supper last night.

The Negro woman working at the drysink turned to face him.

"Why, it's Mister Seth!" Her voice had a *good morning* sound as if she knew him and was pleased to have him drop by.

" 'Morning," he mumbled, embarrassed. He started to draw back, meaning to get himself the hell out of this house he'd intruded into.

"I've been waiting for you, Mister Seth," she said. "Where'd you get off to yesterday?"

"Huh?" He hesitated, looking at her. A small, round-built, middle-aged woman he couldn't recall having ever seen before. Why did she talk to him like she knew him?

"You didn't ever come for your breakfast. But you sit down here now and I'll break some eggs for you."

He *was* hungry. And J.B. and the woman were both out of the house. So why not?

As he seated himself at the kitchen table, she scolded, "You didn't come to breakfast yesterday either, Mister Seth. You didn't come eat yesterday at all."

"I ate in town," he mumbled. "Didn't know you were expecting me."

"You won't get no good food in that town." She set a big iron skillet on the range and began slabbing bacon. Glancing over her shoulder at him, she suggested, "You leave me that shirt a little while, I'll wash it and mend it up for you."

"Can't. Me and this shirt got plans for today."

"You leave that one and I'll fetch you the lend of one of Mister J.B.'s."

"His shirts wouldn't fit me too good," he answered. "And I don't think he'd much cotton to the idea."

She started slapping the slices of bacon into the pan. With her back to him, she said, "Your Pa's a good man, Mister Seth. You ought not fight with him."

He looked at her in surprise. She'd called him by name when she invited him in. He had assumed she knew the stories that went with that name. All the common gossip.

"He ain't my Pa," he said.

"That ain't no way to talk, Mister Seth."

He didn't answer that. Hell, there was no point in it. He was feeling oddly comfortable and at ease here in her kitchen. Why ruin it with talk about J.B.? Instead, he said, "I wish you'd stop calling me *Mister*. It makes me nervous."

Still with her back to him, busy at her work, she told him, "*Mister Seth*—that's what your Pa called you. He said *Mister Seth is come home for a while. You feed him up good now*. That's what he said."

He couldn't believe that. But he didn't want to argue with her. Likely she meant well enough. She'd just put her own meaning on whatever it was J.B.'d told her, he supposed.

She turned to set a plate of cold biscuits on the table, and put down a jam jar to keep it company. Then she looked Seth over critically. "He's sure right. I seen skinnier men than you, but they were mostly dead already. You hurry up and start eating now, you hear?"

"I don't know your name," he said as he reached for a biscuit.

"Amelia. I thought everybody knew Amelia."

"It's a pleasure to meet you, Amelia."

"Pleasure to meet my cooking, you mean." She grinned. "I ain't yet met a man who wasn't pleasured to meet my cooking. You drink milk?"

"No."

She shook her head sadly. As she turned to crack eggs over the skillet, she grumbled, "You cowmen. All them cows all over the place, and I had to plumb holler at Mister J.B. for him to give me a milk cow. Got to have fresh milk and butter for good cooking. Don't none of you cowmen drink milk at all?"

"No," he answered through a mouthful of biscuit.

"All that fresh milk! Can't nobody use it *all* in cooking. Gotta milk that old cow myself too. There ain't none of them cowmen that even knows how to milk a cow. All that work—old cow making milk and me taking it from her—and then half of it goes to waste."

"Still got the calf?"

She nodded.

"You leave some for it?"

She nodded again.

"Maybe you ought to leave more," he suggested.

"Maybe I ought to learn you to drink it. No wonder you got no meat on your bones." Shaking her head again, she scooped a plate full of eggs. She piled on a heap of bacon, and set it in front of him.

"You'll spoil me for trail cooking," he told her.

Her face spread with pleasure as she watched him light into the meal. And when he mopped up the last of the egg with a piece of biscuit, she shoved a wide wedge of pie in front of him.

He looked at it, then at her. With a sigh, he said, "Amelia, what say you and me run away to Texas together? You can make your fortune as a coosie for drovers."

"A *what?*"

"Coosie—cocinero—trail cook."

She laughed. "Me cook for them cowmen that won't drink milk, and don't know nothing but beefsteak and beans? No sir!"

Stretching out his legs, he leaned back lazily in the chair. With a show of disappointment, he said, "It would sure make droving a lot more fun with a cook like you along."

She laughed again, then straightened her face and ordered sternly, "Now you eat that pie before you wither away."

"You got to give me a minute to rest. I'm wore out with eating. You know you can't fatten a calf all . . ."

"Amelia!" It was Chuck's voice, sharp and rasping.

Seth straightened up, suddenly tense, as he heard the footsteps in the hallway. Dammit, did the kid have to show up here and now?

Chuck stepped into the kitchen and halted to gaze narrow-eyed at Seth. "What are you doing here?" he demanded.

"Eating."

"Mister Charles," Amelia said hurriedly, "you sit down while I fix you some breakfast."

"I ain't hungry!" he hollered at her in the same harsh tone he'd used toward Seth.

Coldly, Seth said, "That ain't no way to talk."

56

Amelia interrupted before the boy could answer. "Mister Charles, you sit down and have breakfast with your brother."

"He ain't my brother!"

"I damned well ain't," Seth began. "I'd sooner have a family of coyotes . . ."

"You know your mother was . . ."

Jerking out of the chair, Seth grabbed for the kid. His fingers closed on the front of the silk shirt and his other hand drew back, knotted.

"Stop that!" Amelia shouted. She grabbed a bucket and swung it.

The cold water hit Seth, shocking him enough to stop his fist. Dammit, were they ganging up on him? He let go the kid's shirt and turned toward Amelia. "Don't *you* start ordering me around!"

"Mister Seth, you hush up hollering in my kitchen."

"I'll do my hollering where I damn well please!"

"Not in this house," Chuck screamed at him. "You got no damned business inside this house!"

"You reckon you're already boss of JayBar, little boy?" he snapped back.

"Mister Seth! Mister Charles! You both hush up," Amelia protested. "You sure *act* like brothers."

Seth hesitated. She'd brought sudden memories to him. In a way she was right. He and Jeremy had fought like this, shouting wildly at each other. Only nobody'd ever thought to dump a bucket of water over the two of them. He stood there, soaking wet, suddenly feeling ridiculous with his shirt dripping and his hair plastered against his forehead. He rubbed the back of his hand at the water trickling down his face. Wheeling sharply, he strode through the door and out onto the gallery.

He stopped and wiped at his face with his sleeve. It didn't help much. His shirt was soaked. Hell of a thing to do to a man—dump a bucket of water over him that way. He had to own it had worked though. Amelia had stopped him from a fight he was damned glad he'd escaped.

The dream came into his mind again. Had that been an omen, he wondered. Was he going to end up fighting the kid whether he wanted to or not? And what about the rest of it—where it was himself he'd been beating?

57

"Mister Seth?" Amelia spoke softly.

He turned and looked at her, standing there in the door with concern in her face.

"You'll take sick out here in them wet clothes," she said. "Come on in by the stove."

Quietly, controlling his voice, he said, "Don't order me around, Amelia."

"A person don't always mean to be ordering," she answered. "Sometimes a person means for your own good. That boy in there, he's a good boy. And your Pa is a good man . . ."

"Dammit, Amelia, don't push me. I can't take any more."

"All right," she said softly. She turned then, and disappeared back into the house.

Why the hell couldn't they leave him be? All he wanted was to get his business here done with and to get away again. He didn't want anything from any of them—didn't ask anything of any of them.

But that wasn't true, was it? Reluctantly, he admitted to himself that he'd come back here to beg J.B. to save his damned life.

The breeze was chill on his wet skin. He walked on down the steps into the sunlight and stripped off the shirt. As he wrung it out, he decided he might as well finish the job Amelia had started. Might as well wash it proper. If he built up a fire in Mace's stove and hung it close by, maybe it'd be dry by the time he was ready to ride out and meet Annie Johnson.

That was the one pleasant thought in this whole dismal business—meeting Annie Johnson. He set himself to concentrating on it.

A shame she hadn't been closer to his own age when he'd lived around here, he thought. It would have been real fine to have squired her around. Maybe even to have courted her. He could have shown her the style back then. Could have taken her places in the old man's buggy with the matched strawberry roans high-stepping in front of it.

But he discovered that thinking about Annie was a mixed pleasure. Meeting her was damn fine. But why did it have to be now, with everything else such a mess? He was in a hell of a spot to let himself go getting ideas

58

about courting. Especially when the girl lived almost in the shadow of the JayBar.

But even if it was the wrong time, and a damn fool idea in the first place, it persisted.

Chapter 6

Seth had picked himself another fine-blooded bay geld from among the horses in the corral. And Annie had challenged him to race across the open slope. He'd let her take the lead at the first stride and had held back about half a length behind, admiring the way she rode. It amazed him that anyone could handle a horse well from a sidesaddle. But Annie seemed perfectly at ease, bending low over the sorrel's neck as she urged it for all its speed.

The bay was a stronger, longer-legged horse, though. It could outstride her mount. As they neared the edge of the forest, Seth gave it a touch of the spurs that sent it bounding up to her side.

They drew rein together and laughed together. The run had brought high color to Annie's cheeks and her eyes were bright with the excitement of it. Turning her horse, she called, "Come on!"

He followed as she skirted the forest a ways, then cut into it and onto a game trail so narrow that they had to go single file, ducking low branches. With surprise, he realized where she was leading him. He'd always thought of the pool as a secret place.

He told himself it made sense that other people would know about it. But back when he and Jeremy had been boys exploring these slopes together, they'd counted themselves to be the only white men who'd ever found it. They'd figured themselves far from the known world. It had been a very special and mysterious place. He discovered he still tended to think of it that way.

The trail wound upslope into deep woods and under trees so thick-crowned that sunlight barely reached through them. The horses' hooves fell softly on a deep mat of fir needles, muffled in a twilight silence that seemed too profound to break.

The water was a faint sound, heard long before they

caught sight of it. They came out of the woods, abruptly, right onto the bank of the pond.

There was sunlight here, bright and warm, spilling into the small glade. A fast-running stream tumbled over a low slope of stone, catching sparks of the sun as it splashed into a natural tank.

At the edges, where the water lapped against the rocks, the pool was shallow and as clear as the sky overhead. But toward the middle, it dropped off so deep and dark that it looked as if it might not have any bottom at all.

This was runoff from the snow line far above. But at this time of year, the little traces that carried off spring overflow were dry. The stream poured itself into the pool and disappeared somewhere in unseen depths. That was a part of its mystery.

Looking toward Seth, Annie said softly, "Help me down."

He swung out of the saddle and held a hand up to her. She took it, stepping down with such easy grace that he knew she didn't need help. Holding the reins loosely, she let the mare dip its muzzle into the water. As it drank, she tossed the stirrup over the horn and reached for the cincha.

Seth moved her hand away and loosened it for her. Then he eased the cinchas on his own saddle. When he turned back, she was seated on the rocks at the edge of the pool. He left the horses ground-hitched and sat down beside her.

She was the one who'd chosen to come here. He wondered if she'd had some particular reason. Was this a special place for her, too? He wished he could read whatever thoughts were behind those deep-blue eyes.

She seemed uncertain, as if she weren't quite sure how to break the forest silence either. Glancing around, she picked up a pebble and flung it out, watching it strike the surface, then disappear into the darkness of deep water.

Seth's voice came so softly it was almost a whisper. "When Jeremy and me were boys we used to come up here. We used to say that hole didn't have any bottom. It went straight through the mountain to the middle of the world and came up again on the other side."

Smiling, she said, "Do you suppose it really does?"

"I don't know. I never got down far enough into it to find out."

"Did you try?"

He nodded. "We used to dare each other to see who could go the deepest."

"Weren't you afraid?"

He skimmed a shard of rock over the water, watching it hit and splash as it skidded. It fell suddenly, and disappeared.

"Sometimes," he said. "Sometimes I got down deep enough it seemed like I'd never be able to get to the top again. More than once I figured I was drowned for sure. But somehow I always managed to get back."

He was surprised at his own words. It was the first time he could recall ever admitting to anyone else that he'd been afraid of anything.

Soft-voiced, she said, "Seth, are you back home now to stay?"

Why the hell did she have to ask that? He flung another rock into the water. It broke the surface and sank.

When he didn't answer, she said, "I'm sorry. It isn't any of my business. But—but I've missed you. I hoped you were back for good."

"You know why I left, don't you?"

She nodded slightly. "I've heard talk . . ."

"J.B. *ran* me off. And there isn't anything changed. I'm only back now because . . ." He stopped himself. What was she going to think if she knew he'd run back here to hide from a murder warrant? He mumbled, "I'm back but I'll be pulling out again. Same as before."

He tugged the tobacco sack out of his pocket. As he busied himself with building a smoke, he wondered just what it was that she'd heard. He remembered the way that kid had tried to brace him back at the corral. From what he'd said, there were some damned ugly rumors. He lit the cigarette, then asked, "Annie, what do they say about me around here now?"

"Nothing."

Chuck had gotten his crazy ideas from somewhere, he thought. "They must be saying something."

"You think you're the only thing that ever happened in Long County, Seth Yarborough? Why since you left," she tallied on her fingers, "they've built a new railroad depot, the Kellers' barn got struck by lightning and burnt to the ground, Louise Stanhope married a man from Boston, Mister Langer's cat has had more kittens than you could count in . . ."

"Look, I'm not sulling over what folks might be calling me," he told her. "It's just that this kid—J.B.'s new stepson—has got some kind of wild idea that I came back here to kill him and I'm wondering where . . ."

"You? To kill him! Oh, Seth!" She sounded hurt. And when he looked up, her eyes were serious and troubled.

He was sorry he'd let that slip out. It wasn't anything to talk about. Not here and not to her. But somehow with her he kept saying things—not the angry way he'd snap back at other people—but *real* things, the true thoughts that were in his mind.

"He just doesn't know you, Seth," she said.

"Nobody around here does," he mumbled.

"I do."

He looked at her again, wondering what she meant by that. Or what she *thought* she meant. She was smiling slightly. It was a small secretive woman-smile. It seemed almost inviting. He rose to his knees, starting to reach toward her. But she drew back from his hand.

"Seth!" The way she said it left no question. Her smile hadn't been an invitation.

He stopped himself and sat back on his heels, feeling ashamed. She was no saloon girl. Why the hell did he do things like that? Dammit, she muddled his thoughts. But he knew one thing for sure: He wanted her to stay here with him, not run off scared, or worse. Just talking with her was pleasant enough—too pleasant for him to chance frightening her away.

"I'm sorry," he said. It sounded ridiculous and inadequate.

She lifted her head and the sunlight caught on her face, brightening her eyes. With a light laugh, she said, "A solemn and horrible oath, Seth."

He grinned then, at ease again, admiring how she understood things. "I make mistakes. If I do, you stop me. Put up with me till I get used to being here."

"You've been away a long time."

He nodded. It seemed like a hell of a long time. Sometimes it seemed as if he'd never been a part of her kind of life. He wasn't sure he remembered how to court a girl proper. Wasn't sure he'd ever known.

"There's going to be partying at Tatums' a week from Saturday," she was saying. "Will you take me, Seth?"

For a moment he just stared at her, as startled as if she'd slapped him. Then he grinned again. "Hell, yes!"

She turned away suddenly, color rising in her cheeks. And he muttered a silent curse at himself. Couldn't he say two things in a row without one of them being wrong? He mumbled, "I'm sorry, Annie. I guess my language isn't . . ."

"My ears aren't *that* tender." She looked at him sidewise. "I just—well, I—I never asked a man to a dance before. You must think I'm awfully forward."

"I think you're wonderful."

Her blush deepened and her eyes turned away again. She seemed somehow pleased and sad at the same time. He hoped desperately that hadn't been another wrong thing to say. This talk had gotten too serious, he thought. He wanted to hear her laugh again, in that light, care-free way. As he searched for words, he poked a finger at the pebbles in the dry run.

She reached to touch one of the ones he'd turned. "Look, Seth. There's a stone egg."

He picked it up. "You reckon it'd hatch?"

She nodded.

"Into what?"

"A little hill that would grow up into a mountain."

He skipped the egg-pebble across the pool. It splashed, then sank into the dark hollow. He told her, "It'll go through and hatch on the other side. Grow a Colorado mountain over there in China or somewhere like that."

"As big as Bloodyhead?" she asked.

"Bigger."

"I'd like to see that."

"When it's full-grown, I'll fetch it back here for you to take a look at it."

"The whole mountain?"

"Sure," he said. "The whole mountain. Roots and all."

"That's a long way to haul a mountain—all the way from China. Maybe it would be easier if I went there to see it."

"No trouble, ma'am. I'll bring the mountain to you."

"It could set down its roots here then, and keep right on growing," she said. And she was looking at him as if she meant to read deep into his thoughts.

He turned his face away. Gazing at the dark water, he said, "No. That wouldn't work."

"Then I'll go to the mountain. Wherever it takes root, I'll go to it there."

Could she mean as much by that as it seemed, he wondered. Was she just passing time in talking, or was there more to it than that? She'd come up here alone with him—but she didn't want him to touch her. What was it she did want?

"It's getting late, Seth," she said suddenly—hurriedly. "I've got to get started home."

"Now?"

She nodded, almost as if she were eager to go. And he thought maybe he'd been wrong to find anything at all in the talk they'd made together. Maybe she was just being sociable, making conversation.

Rising, he offered her his hand. She took it and stood up. For a moment, she was very close to him and her hand was wrapped tightly around his. But then her fingers opened and slipped away.

She was smiling as she said lightly, "If I'm not home for supper my folks'll start to worry about me."

"Likely they'd come hunting for you?" He tried to match her tone.

"Likely."

"Your Pa got a shotgun?"

"Of course."

He grinned at her, hoping to sound as teasing as she did. "Then I reckon I'd better get you on home."

As they rode they talked about trivial things. And they were laughing together again when they reached sight of the Johnson place. As they drew rein, side by side, he asked, "You likely to be riding up to that park again?"

"I'm likely to be riding up there every day."

"Then you'll be running into me every day, as long as I'm around here."

"How long will that be?"

"At least till Saturday a week," he said. Then, his voice serious, "Annie, if you want to change your mind about going to that dance with me . . ."

"I've been waiting a lot of years for you to take me to a dance, Seth Yarborough, and I'm not going to change my mind now."

"Waiting?"

She smiled self-consciously, her cheeks reddening, as she wheeled the mare and started toward the house. When she was gone from his sight, he turned the bay and set it into an exuberant run.

A week from Saturday. That seemed like a hell of a long time away. Even tomorrow afternoon seemed a long wait. He wondered what a man would have to do—and be—to entitle himself to ride all the way to the house with her. What kind of a man would her folks welcome to call on her? Not Seth Yarborough, he figured. But he'd call at the door for her a week from Saturday whether they liked it or not. Somehow, he'd lay hands on a rig for the evening. And get himself some decent clothes, too. He wasn't sure where or how, but he'd damned well find a way.

He headed back along the ridge at an amble. The bay was chirruping at the bit cricket and the curb was jangling at each bob of its head. His spurs jangled too. The big Mexican rowels were made to ring like bells. It was pleasant music to match good thoughts.

In a while he'd begun to whistle to himself as he relaxed in the saddle, enjoying the scents of the mountains—the pine and spruce, the cool rocks and sweet water. Good land. Really something to look at.

A man could get damned serious about a girl like Annie Johnson real easy. And maybe it could be made to work out . . .

He stopped whistling suddenly, jerking rein on the bay so hard that he set it back on its haunches. He'd seen a rider—just a glimpse, just for an instant—a man moving through the forest. And it had looked like Jeremy. But Jeremy was six years dead and buried.

Somebody else, he told himself. Most likely just one of the JayBar hands. He didn't put any faith in the stories of ghosts. A man didn't ride out again, once he'd had six feet of dirt piled on his face.

He touched spurs to the bay's flanks, heading it on down the ridge, feeling coldly uncomfortable, as if there were hidden eyes watching him. He told himself it was just the cool of the shadow he'd ridden into. As he reached the bottom of the ravine, he spurred the horse into a lope, and tried to turn his thoughts back to

Annie, hoping to recapture that pleasant feeling he'd had a few moments before.

The horse reared suddenly, screaming.

Above its cry of pain, Seth heard the crack of a rifle echoing in the ravine. He grabbed at the reins as the horse twisted under him. It was up high, forehooves pawing air frantically. He tried throwing his weight forward, but it was up too high. He could feel it losing balance. It was going over backward. He flung himself away from the saddle, sprawling on the ground as the horse fell.

As he glanced over his shoulder, he could see it flail, trying to rise again. The second rifle shot hit dirt close to his face.

Scrambling his legs under him, he ran. His hand wrapped itself around the butt of the Colt, jerking it. As he threw himself down behind the cover of a boulder, he swung the gun muzzle up toward the ridge.

He let the hammer slap down once, knowing it was useless. He wasn't aiming and sure not likely to hit. He had no idea what to aim at. But he had to do something.

The gun bucked in his hand. Damned waste of a cartridge. He gazed at the face of the ravine wall, but there was nothing to be seen. The mass of rough rock was overgrown with brush along its upper edge and was dark with its own shadow.

The third rifle shot splatted against the boulder, stinging his face with chips.

He jumped back, pulling in his legs, huddling close to the stone. That time he thought he'd seen a wisp of smoke. Hard to be sure, though.

He wanted to look again, but that last shot had been too close. He felt damned uncomfortable at the idea of showing himself.

Fingering the Colt, he considered. The rim was beyond range of the handgun. But the ambusher couldn't get another shot at him as long as neither one of them moved. He was pinned pretty good here, not a bit of cover he could reach without an exposed run. He didn't dare try it. Not now. Maybe not until the shadows blended into night. Or the sharpshooter decided to try from a different spot.

Leaning his cheek against the cool of the rock, he

waited, listening and wondering. Who wanted him dead that bad?

He could make a probable list easy enough. J.B.'s new wife was willing to pay a thousand dollars if he'd leave. Maybe she'd pay that much to have him killed. Her crazy son had tried to provoke a shooting. Maybe the kid would be willing to try an ambush too. And then there was J.B. himself.

It was a hell of a thought. A damned ugly thought that made him feel a bit sick. He rubbed at his face with the back of the hand that held the gun. In a way he could understand the old man running him off after Jeremy was killed. But this? Shooting at him from ambush—his own father?

Angrily, he told himself that J.B. wasn't his father. Why did he keep thinking of him that way? Why the hell did he keep expecting the old man to think of him as a son? He wasn't J.B.'s son—he was the one who'd killed J.B.'s son.

He edged his head up a bit, trying to see that spot up on the ridge. And lead slammed into the rock, spooking him back again.

Silent, uncertain, he listened for some sound that would tell him the ambusher was trying to move in on him.

Goddammit, go ahead and kill me—it won't change anything—it won't bring Jeremy back—what the hell do you want from me anyhow?

He had to know. Maybe he'd get himself killed, but he had to try to find out who was behind that rifle.

He moved cautiously to study the ravine wall. There was a dry water run angling down it, a shallow ragged gash in the rock that looked like it might offer footholds. And if he could make the quick dash to the ravine wall and flatten himself there, the ambusher would have a rough time trying to fire along the wall at him.

The rifle cracked again, spattering more chips of rock. Whoever was up there was no professional killer, Seth decided as he pulled back. Maybe a good hunter of animals, but not much of a man-killer. He'd had a perfect target for those first two shots, but he'd missed. And now he was shooting too quick. Seemed anxious and nervous. Well, that was just fine.

Thumbing open the gate of the Colt, he replaced the

round he'd fired. Then he picked up a fist-sized chunk of rubble.

Stay nervous, Mister.

Crouching, he sent the rock skittering across the ground.

The ambusher sent a quick shot at the dust it raised. And Seth ran.

He flung himself up against the wall of rock, pressing his body into the shallow water run. The rifle snapped again, spraying gravel near his heels.

Twisting his head, he judged the outcropping of the ravine wall to offer fair cover. He dropped the Colt back into his holster and grabbed a handful of jutting rock. Carefully, he began to climb.

His boots jarred loose rubble that clattered down the rock, sounding too damned loud in the stillness. He hauled himself up to a secure foothold and paused to grab breath.

There was another sound. Tense, he listened. It came from above—a stealthy rustle of brush. The ambusher knew what he was up to. Was the man moving in to get a good shot as he clambered up the rock?

No—the sound was moving away. Nervous enough to run, he thought. Spooked and running now. And, dammit, he *had* to identify the man. Recklessly, he scrambled on up the water run.

Brush rustled again, but there was nothing furtive about the sound now. And as Seth dragged himself over the edge, he heard a horse. It snorted, somewhere in the trees, then broke into a gallop.

Had the bushwhacker gotten away? Or maybe he'd only whipped up the horse as a decoy. Maybe he was still waiting in the woods, looking for another shot.

The revolver in his hand, Seth crouched low to keep from skylighting himself. He scanned the trees. Was that something moving? He snapped a shot at it. But he felt sure it had only been a shadow stirred by the breeze.

The sun was sinking low, and a chill wind spilled over the lip of the ravine. It whispered through the trees. He shivered as it brushed across his face. Hunkering there, he listened. Things scurried through the grass—tiny feet hurrying, small bodies rustling whatever they brushed against. But nothing that sounded like a man afoot trying **to** move quietly. Nothing like the sweaty scent of a

69

human body. He couldn't even hear the horse's hooves any longer.

With a deep, miserable disappointment, he decided his first guess had been right. The ambusher had gotten away.

And he wasn't likely to come back now either. He'd been nervous to begin with, and scared enough to run out when his quarry turned back at him. Now that he knew Seth was alert, he wasn't likely to try crawling through the growing darkness to get another shot. No, he'd bide his time, looking to sneak up unexpected and try bushwhacking again.

Goddammit, who was he!

It was already deep twilight here on the rock rim, and too dark under the trees to hunt for sign. No chance of trailing the man. No chance of finding out—not until he tried again.

Seth picked up a loose rock and hurled it angrily down the face of the ravine. He heard it hit and tumble, taking a shower of rubble with it. A lot of good that did.

With a sigh, he holstered the Colt and started the climb down again.

Chapter 7

The horse was gone. Not much of the twilight glow from above reached down into the ravine, but there was enough for Seth to determine that the horse had scrambled to its feet and run. Probably while he was pinned behind that boulder with all his attention on the rifleman. Well, at least the animal wasn't dead or hurt too bad to move. But it was a damned long walk from here to the ranch. Resigning himself to the fact that he was afoot, he set out.

As he walked, he listened. He felt certain that the ambusher wouldn't be doubling back to try again, but his right hand hung open, tense, near the butt of the Colt. Hell of a thing to be on the wrong end of a rifle, hunted like a game animal. Hell of a thing to know it might happen again, suddenly, without warning.

Had it been J.B. looking at him over that gunsight? Would J.B. have been nervous enough to miss the first shot? Likely the old man could lay his sights on a person as easily as he could take a strap to one.

The woman wouldn't be doing her own killing, he figured. She'd pay for the job. That ambusher hadn't been a professional, but maybe she couldn't get one on such short order. She might have made a deal with one of the ranch hands.

Or had it been Chuck? That notion didn't set well. The kid might be short-fused, without much good sense, but was he a back-shooter? Seth didn't like that idea at all. Hell, the kid had been willing to make his stand face to face yesterday. A damn fool maybe, but with guts enough for a kid his age. Didn't seem likely he'd turn to bushwhacking.

Who else? he asked himself. Was there any reason someone else in these parts might want to be rid of Seth Yarborough once and for all? He thought back six years and more, cataloging people he'd known. He'd fought plenty of them, made himself enemies with enough of them. Usually it had been word flinging or fist fights, though there had been a couple of gun scrapes the old man'd had to square for him. But nothing serious—not serious enough to bushwhack a man for.

And then he remembered how close he'd come to drawing a gun against Bud Tatum back there in the saloon. Was there someone around here who'd been storing up an old hate for *him* that same way?

Ranging back through memories, he recalled the last fight he and Jeremy'd had with each other. That had been in the street, right down there in Jubilee, with half the town watching. He could remember the heat of the sun on his back, the smell of the dust, and the shouting. He could almost taste the blood again.

Jeremy'd caught him a good one in the mouth. Chipped a tooth and cut his lip. The tooth had ached a while afterward, but he'd kept it washed with whiskey and eventually the aching had stopped. That didn't always work, did it?

They'd been fighting over a girl that time, deciding the hard way who was entitled to ask her to the end-of-roundup dance. Back then it had seemed important, but now he wasn't even sure which girl it had been. He knew now he'd just been bucking Jeremy, trying to prove he could take the girl away from him. Damn fool silly business. Sure as hell nothing you'd kill a man about. But folks had whispered it around that she was one reason he'd shot Jeremy.

A girl, an inheritance, years of wrangling with each other—folks figured those added up to reason enough for a man to kill his brother. Or rather, to kill a man who wasn't really his brother. They'd made up their minds and spread their talk, and how could he have explained different to them?

He couldn't explain the terse, sharp way he'd answered questions, or the way he'd stood in dry-eyed silence through the funeral and then turned his back on the people who tried to offer kind words. He couldn't have told them how damned scared he was, alone and lost without Jeremy. He couldn't say he'd cried out his misery there in the woods, with Jeremy's head in his arms. He couldn't tell them anything—not the townspeople—not J.B.

So he'd turned his back and let them talk. And when he couldn't take any more of it . . .

Mace had warned him about the talk, even before the funeral. Word for word, Mace had repeated the worst of the rumors to him. So he'd known what they were really thinking, those kind-faced mourners who'd offered him their condolences. And on the silent ride back to the empty house, he'd been damned sure J.B. was thinking the same thing.

The memory was vivid, alive in his mind again. He recalled that the lamps were cold, and only the dull twilight sky beyond the windows had given form to them as they faced each other in the kitchen. He'd been heading on through the house to go to his room, but J.B. had stepped in front of him, stopping him.

"There's talk going around," the old man had said, his granite voice sounding hollow in the darkness. "They're saying you *meant* to kill Jeremy."

He'd been expecting that accusation, and he'd thought he was ready to face it. He'd been wrong.

At that moment, suddenly, he'd felt that if his own father believed it there was no damned point in even trying to make a denial. The words he'd planned all seemed futile. He was cornered and attacked. Alone, he only knew one way to protect himself—hit first and hit hard—hit to hurt.

Angrily, he'd snapped back, "What if I did!"

And that had been the end of it. The end of everything. J.B. had wheeled to stride away. When he'd come back a moment later, it was to fling the money down on the table. A hundred dollars in gold.

"Take your pick of the horses and get the hell out of my sight. Don't ever set foot in these mountains again."

Unanswering, Seth had gone. He'd taken the money and he'd walked out to saddle a horse and ride away, still in the suit he'd worn to the funeral. He'd left everything else. And he told himself he was damned glad to be done with JayBar. He'd thought then that nothing could ever drive him back within sight of the Yarborough land again. With Jeremy dead, there was no place for him here.

But he had come back. He'd come here now looking

73

to J.B. to save his life. And now somebody here was trying to kill him.

It seemed like he'd been walking a hell of a long time. The moon had risen to spill its thin, pale light in patches through the trees. He stopped and seated himself on a windfallen log, resting his head in his hands. God, but he was tired. Nigh too tired to go any farther.

He closed his eyes, and Jeremy was in his mind again. Jeremy'd been two years older than him, a fair bit taller and heavier. Built like a Yarborough, and with the ox-strength that was natural to them. That hadn't made their fights bad matches though. Seth had learned young that his advantage was in being quick, and he'd learned it well. He could hold his own against Jeremy, sometimes beat him. He'd sure meant to that day. But Mace had shown up and pried them apart with the fight unfinished and the question unsettled.

They'd both sulked afterward. That was the way it usually went—with Mace stopping the fight before it was settled and the two of them brooding for a while. But then they always made it up again.

Mace had suggested they pack out on a hunting trip. That was the surest, quickest way to get them over their sulking. Get them off together, out of sight of the ranch house, away from the old man, and they'd be friends again.

It always worked. By the time they'd made their first night's camp, the whole fight was out of mind. Seth was glad for that—glad he'd been friends with Jeremy again before it happened. . . .

"Goddammit," he muttered aloud. What the hell was he doing sitting here brooding over things years past? There wasn't anything to be got from thinking it all through again, remembering all the misery.

He rubbed his face, then looked at his own shadow stretching out in the grass in front of him. The moon was shining straight onto his back. He realized he was sitting there like a bottle on a stump, only he was a damn sight bigger and easier a target than a bottle. And that ambusher *could* have circled back.

He headed into the trees, not running but walking fast, feeling scared and ashamed of the feeling. *A tough hand, that Seth Yarborough—a hardcase.* He might have sold that idea to a lot of others, but he hadn't yet managed to sell it to himself. He listened intently as he walked, but he heard only the night sounds, caught only the scents of the forest.

His hands were sweaty. He wiped them on his thighs and cursed himself for a fool. If anyone had been tracking him, looking to get another shot at him, it would have been done by now. He wouldn't have been let sit on that log so long, lost in his own thoughts.

When he finally reached the slope overlooking the ranch buildings, he paused. Damned long walk. He ached from it. To judge by the stars, it was around midnight now. He wondered if the horse had come back.

Well, if it had wandered in already, nobody'd bothered to stay up wondering why his saddle was empty or how the horse had gotten injured. The bunkhouse was dark. From the back side, so was the mansion. Its windows looked dead, its white-painted woodwork as stark as dry bones in the moonlight. Everybody asleep, quiet and peaceful, he thought to himself. Or was one of them lying awake, planning another ambush?

He plodded on down toward the bunkhouse. Mace had probably been bedded and asleep for hours. He tried to edge the door open silently, but it squealed on its iron hinges.

"Who's that?" he heard Mace mumble thickly. "Seth?"

"Yeah, didn't mean to waken you."

In the moonlight that spilled past him through the doorway, he could see Mace prop up on one arm, shaking his head and squinting. He glanced around, orienting himself, then closed the door and felt for the edge of the table. His hand found it, then the chair. Seating himself, he started to pull off a boot.

"Where've you been?" Mace asked him. "J.B.'s been raising hell for you."

Seth paused, looking into the darkness toward his voice. Again, he wondered if it could have been the old man behind that rifle.

"Yeah?" he said. "When did he get back from town?"

"Dunno. He was home when I came in for the day."

"When was that?"

Mace hesitated. "Couple hours after sunset. Why?"

"Just wondering. I reckon he's bedded by now."

"J.B.? Maybe not. Sometimes he sits up at that desk of his half the night. You want to see him *now?*"

Seth put his foot on the floor and kicked his heel back down into the boot. Rising, he said, "Yeah, I think I do."

He heard Mace grunt as he closed the door behind him. Did he really want to face J.B. now, he asked himself. Well, he had to do it sometime. Why not now? Do it while that ambush was still strong in his mind. Accuse the old man of having tried to bushwhack him. It wasn't a very pleasant prospect, and couldn't be sure it really had been J.B. behind that rifle. But he wanted to face him with the accusation—see how *he* liked being called a back-shooter.

As he turned the corner of the house, he could see lamp-glow from that same front window. Mace was right, the old man was still in the study. Going over the books, pleasuring himself by counting his money?

He moved quietly to the window and looked in. The wingbacked chair was empty. J.B. was in the swivel chair, his arms on the desk with his head resting on them. The lamp at his side was turned low, casting long shadows, leaving the corners of the room in darkness.

Asleep, Seth thought, and he hesitated, almost turning away. But he asked himself *why?* Was he afraid to waken J.B.? Was he looking for an excuse to back out?

He rapped his knuckles on the windowsill.

J.B.'s shoulders jerked. As he lifted his head to look toward the window, Seth stepped in.

"Don't you ever use doors?" the old man mumbled, sounding still half asleep.

For no reason he could figure, the softness of the carpet underfoot annoyed Seth. Striding, his heels sinking deep into it, he walked to the desk and jammed his hands into his pockets.

His voice came coldly, edged with defiance. "Just saw Mace. He said you wanted to see me."

J.B. looked him down critically. "I hear you went into town."

"Yeah."

In his mind, Seth worded out the accusation he'd come here to make. But he couldn't speak it out. Dammit, why not? J.B.'d never held off on *him*.

His glance caught the cut glass decanter on the table. He picked it up, jerked the stopper and took a long drag. Smooth, easy-drinking brandy. Expensive stuff. Everything around this damned place was expensive.

It wasn't until he'd put the decanter down and wiped at his mouth with the back of his hand that J.B. spoke to him again.

"You got *any* manners left?"

"No." Why the hell should he have? Man doesn't need indoors manners trail-herding beeves. He dropped into the winged chair, hooking one leg over the armrest, and gazed insolently at J.B.

His resolution to accuse the old man seemed to have faded. Or had he just lost his nerve? He wasn't sure. Reaching over his shoulder, he picked up the decanter and drank from it again.

"Mace tell you I wanted you to stay on the ranch?" J.B. asked.

Seth nodded.

"But you went to town anyway?"

"Yeah."

"Why?"

"To buy a drink."

The old man sighed. "Well, at least you didn't get into trouble there this time."

Why should I have? Seth asked himself. The trouble had all been bunched up here at JayBar waiting for him. He grunted, "I've met your new son. Feisty kid, but he don't *look* much like a Yarborough."

J.B. rose to his feet. Using his height, he towered over Seth. He looked like a thunderhead, about to start spitting lightning. But whatever he'd meant to say, he stopped himself and sat down again.

He eyed Seth, then said, "I've been in to see my lawyer."

"Mace told me." Seth tasted the brandy again, then slumped a little deeper into the chair, cradling the decanter on his chest. He almost wished the old man would bust loose at him. It would make this easier. If he were angrier, he could speak his piece against the old man.

"I've given Grayling a free hand in this," J.B. told him. "He's going out to Horseshoe himself. He'll get the straight of the story and find out what's to be done. He's a good man. If anybody can straighten out this mess you've got yourself into . . ."

"*You* want to know what happened?"

". . . he can."

It was as if the old man hadn't even heard him. As

77

if he didn't *want* to listen. Well, to hell with him. It didn't matter what had really happened. The truth was what a man decided it was. And J.B. had made his decision a long time ago. Talk wouldn't make any difference.

He tried another swallow of the brandy and looked at J.B., wondering why the old man hadn't changed in six years. Everybody else had. Annie Johnson had stopped being a brat and had turned into a lovely young woman. Mace had begun getting gray and had become the ranch foreman. Seth himself had turned saddle tramp and killed another man. Why the hell didn't J.B. change?

". . . He'll wire me," the old man was saying. "Until this thing is cleared up, Seth, I don't want you setting foot off JayBar again. For God's sake, *don't* go back into town."

Seth lifted a hand and tried to snap his fingers. It didn't work, so he said it, "Snap—stay, snap—go."

"What's the matter with you, Seth?"

"You think I'd go into town and start trouble on purpose? You think I'd go in to kill me a man for breakfast? Maybe I should start notching my gunbutt . . ." He shook his head slowly. "Not enough yet. Only two notches—one for Jeremy, one for Wilson."

"Seth . . ."

"Maybe I should kill me a couple more tomorrow. Too late to get it done tonight." His voice sounded thick, dull in his own ears. It occurred to him maybe he'd drunk too much of that brandy. But what the hell did it matter?

J.B. stood up, looming over him again. "Goddammit, Seth!"

"What?"

"Look, boy, I'm trying to help you."

Like hell, he thought. *If I didn't have hold of your fine family name that's so respected in this state, you'd be plenty happy to see me hanged. It'd save you the trouble of putting a bullet in my back.*

But he couldn't say it out loud. He still wasn't angry enough or drunk enough to speak his piece. He tried the brandy again, only it didn't help. Suddenly, he wasn't angry at all. Just weary and miserable. Too damned tired to fight any longer.

He looked up at J.B., tall, looming, his hard-set face

78

shadowed in the dim light. The same—exactly the same —as he had been six years ago.

Thin-voiced, almost pleading, Seth asked, "Pa, what is it you want from me?"

The old man's gaze moved over him, from his face to the brandy decanter he held on his chest, to the gun he wore, to the shabby Levi's and scuffed boots. Slowly, hoarsely, he answered, "Nothing."

Seth watched him turn his back and seat himself at the desk. Then he let his eyes close.

Six years was a long time. Everything changed in six years. Why the hell didn't the old man?

When he opened them again, he almost expected to see J.B. standing over him with that belt in his hands, ready to strap him again. But the old man was still at the desk with his back turned. He seemed intent on the paper that lay in front of him.

Seth asked himself what the hell he was waiting here for. He stirred, and discovered he'd definitely put down too much of the brandy. It was awkward getting out of that deep chair and onto his feet. But J.B. paid him no attention as he stood up and headed toward the window. He braced a hand against the frame to steady himself.

"Seth."

Startled, he looked back over his shoulder, suddenly as tense as if the old man's voice had been the cock of a gun hammer.

J.B. faced him now, but the lamplight was behind him. Seth saw him only as a bulking shadow. What did the old man want, he wondered. What else was to be said? He discovered he still had the decanter gripped in his hand. So that was it—he was walking off with the old man's brandy. He started to put it back on the table.

Sighing, J.B. said, "Take it if you want it." Then he turned away.

Seth looked at the decanter uncertainly. He shrugged and climbed on through the window, taking it with him.

Chapter 8

The same dream plagued Seth again—that dream of slamming his fist at Chuck, and at himself. It was a damned ugly dream. But when he managed to break free of it, he decided being awake wasn't much of an improvement. He felt aching, miserably rotten, inside and out. For a long while he lay still, his eyes closed, hoping the feeling would go away, or at least ease up.

That talk with J.B. last night was vague in his mind, but he knew he hadn't done what he'd intended. He hadn't accused J.B. of trying to kill him. He was glad now he hadn't. *Back-shooter* was a mean name to put to a man. Hell of a name to put to him if he was innocent.

He heard someone moving, and smelled coffee cooking. His voice thick in his throat, he mumbled, "Mace?"

"Huh? You awake?"

"No, but I'm trying." He rubbed at his face and forced open his eyes. The world looked fuzzy. The flame of the lamp on the bureau wasn't very high, but its blur cut into his eyes. He pressed them closed again, cursing the old man's brandy. But he had a notion the liquor wasn't the only reason he felt this way.

Well, there wasn't any escape. If he tried sleeping again, he'd probably find himself back in that same damned dream. Stiffly, he propped himself up on his elbow and squinted at Mace. "You spare me a cup of that coffee?"

"You want breakfast in bed, too?" the foreman snapped back.

Seth stopped himself from answering in kind. If there was anything he didn't want this morning, it was an argument. He closed his eyes and sunk his head down onto the quilts again, muttering, "Never mind."

Was Mace still brooding over that business with Lucille Yarborough, he wondered. He had a feeling he ought to

80

say something apologetic, make it up somehow. But that was a thing he'd never found it easy to do. Hell, he'd damned rarely been able to do it at all.

He thought again about Jeremy. That had been one of the really fine things about him. You didn't have to come right out and make an apology to Jeremy in so many words. He'd understood anyway.

"Here."

Seth opened his eyes and saw Mace holding out a full coffee cup toward him. Gratefully, he accepted it. Mace had always been decent about putting up with him and his ways back then. Maybe he still was. Maybe he'd understand now.

The coffee was plenty hot. Strong, too. He felt it sear down his throat and hit with a jolt. Blinking, he looked at Mace again.

The foreman poured a cup for himself and settled at the table. He sat there expectantly. And after a moment, he grunted, "Well?"

"Well?" Seth repeated.

"Well, you didn't chouse yourself awake just for my coffee."

"No," he owned. Mace didn't sound so angry now, but he didn't sound any too friendly either. Seth set himself to the job and finally said, "Look, I'm sorry about that trouble yesterday. And the night before."

Mace took another swallow of his coffee. He looked at Seth curiously from the corner of his eye. "Never heard you say that before."

"What?"

"That you were sorry for anything you done."

Dammit, what did he mean by that? Uncomfortable under his gaze, Seth dug out the makings and began to build a smoke. It gave him something to look busy at. He wondered if Mace was going to make an issue out of all this.

He got the cigarette lit, dragged on it, then turned toward Mace again. The foreman was still watching him expectantly.

"Well?"

"Well what?" Mace grunted.

Seth rubbed at his face. What the hell did Mace want him to do, get down on his knees? He muttered, "If you got a burr under your tongue, spit it out."

"Me? *You're* the one that's boiling with the lid on."

Hell, maybe he was right, Seth thought. The memory of that ambush was still a taut knot in his mind. He still had to know who had been behind that rifle. But he didn't feel like talking about it. For a long moment, he twisted at the thoughts in his mind. He didn't want to believe it had been J.B. And any mention of Lucille might trigger Mace's anger again. Finally, he asked, "This new stepson of J.B.'s, what's he like?"

"Why?"

"I want to know, dammit!"

"All right, all right . . ."

Seth drew a breath, fighting his own anger. "I'm sorry, Mace."

The foreman looked at him curiously again.

"The kid's been prodding me ever since I got here," Seth offered in explanation. "I'd just like to know more about him."

"That ain't all of it," Mace said with a firm certainty.

Seth shook his head. He leaned back against the wall, feeling damned weary again. He was tired of fighting— with other people—with himself. "Yeah," he mumbled. "Truth is, somebody took a couple of shots at me yesterday."

"You think it was Charlie-boy?"

"I don't know."

Mace considered. Sounding reluctant, he said, "That's one damned ornery kid, Seth. And he sure as hell ain't got no use for you."

"I found that out already."

Slowly, as if he were measuring out each word before he used it, Mace continued, "That's a *mean* kid, and sneaky too. He's bossy and spoilt rotten. Acts like he thinks he owns this place already. I sure wouldn't put it past him to try a thing like that."

"Back-shooting? It don't fit with what I've seen of him," Seth said. He felt reluctant to take Mace's opinion of the kid. "He was game to face me, first day I got here."

"You only seen him a couple of times. I seen him ever since he came here. I tell you he's an ornery, sneaky little sonofabitch!"

"Being ornery don't make him a back-shooter."

"It was *your* idea. *You're* the one said the kid tried to bushwhack you," Mace snapped back at him.

"I don't know who it was. I just thought *maybe* it was the kid. Could have been somebody else."

"Who?"

He knew he damned well couldn't say Lucille Yarborough without Mace exploding in his face. Instead, he mumbled, "Might have been J.B.."

That startled Mace. He studied Seth thoughtfully for a long, silent moment, then nodded in agreement.

Seth found himself about to protest again. He didn't want it to have been J.B. He wanted Mace to argue against that—to give him a lot of good solid reasons why it *couldn't* have been J.B.

But Mace answered, "Could be it was him. He's been broody as hell since he buried Jeremy. You never knowed the things he said against you after you left."

Seth rubbed the back of his hand across his mouth, then asked, "And since I come back?"

"What do you think?"

"Yeah," he mumbled. He figured he knew the gist of it.

"The way Jeremy died—it's been eating at him all these years," Mace said. "Might be he's decided he owes you a damn sight more'n he gave you."

Seth gazed down into the coffee cup. He couldn't talk about this any more. He couldn't listen to it. He had to fight back the urge to attack—to beat Mace into admitting that it was all a damned lie. Only maybe it wasn't.

Mace studied him a moment longer, then gulped down the last of his coffee and got to his feet. He shot Seth a grin. "I got to get to work. You take my advice, you'll forget this whole thing. Likely whoever it was just meant to give you a scare."

"Sure," Seth muttered, knowing that wasn't so.

"You ought to get more sleep," Mace told him. "You look like hell."

He glanced up. Well, at least Mace was over his sull. "You're not the Queen of the May yourself," he muttered.

Mace chuckled as he walked out.

Leaning his head back against the wall, Seth closed his eyes. But he didn't intend to sleep again. Not with that dream waiting for him. Dammit, but his head ached.

He told himself Mace was all wrong about J.B. Wrong about the kid, too. Chuck might be feisty, but he wasn't the kind of ugly sneak Mace made him out to be. Likely the boy'd gone around trying to act the man with Mace and

83

got him rankled. Mace was getting damned touchy as he got older. He'd probably misunderstood the kid. Damned easy for a person to misunderstand a kid like that one.

After a while, Seth got up and pulled the coffeepot back over the fire. While it heated, he went into the yard and ducked his head under the pump. That helped the ache. When he'd finished dressing, he laced the dregs of the coffee with what was left of the brandy and gulped it down. That helped, too. There were muscles in his legs that were sore from the walk yesterday, and his shoulders still felt stiff, but the ache in his head was about gone.

Leaning against the door jamb, he looked across the yard at the big house. He wished he could see that kid on peaceable terms, try talking quiet and sensibly with him. If he could keep from getting his own hackles up, it might be Chuck would hold still and talk. But bedamned if he knew how to go about trying it.

There were cooking scents in the air. He looked at the smoke curling up from the kitchen chimney, and remembered that he hadn't eaten since yesterday morning. The whole family was probably at home right now. But there was a kitchen window onto the back yard, and it was open. Not like he'd have to go through the rest of the house. Shoving his hands into his pockets, he ambled toward the window.

Amelia seemed to be alone in the kitchen, busy at her work. He watched her through the window a moment, then rapped on the sill.

Startled, she spun around. And smiled broadly as she recognized him.

"You reckon a drover might beg breakfast here without he got into a fight?" he asked, grinning.

"You come on inside. I got a whole mess of food just waiting for somebody to come along and eat it."

"Where's the boss this morning?"

"Mister J.B.?"

He nodded.

"He took the Missus out to visit in the buggy," she answered. "And Mister Charles ain't come down yet. It's awful quiet around here."

"Not too quiet for me," he said as he hoisted himself over the windowsill.

Amelia laughed. "That any way to come inside?"

"I don't use doors any more," he muttered, reminded of

that business with J.B. last night. Dammit, he shouldn't have gone there when he was too tired to think straight. Shouldn't have got himself drunk. There seemed to be a hell of a lot of *shouldn't haves* in his life.

"You set yourself down while I put the bacon on," Amelia was saying. "You sure you don't want a glass of milk?"

"Real sure."

She started cussing him again for the way drovers ate. He leaned back in the chair, relaxing, enjoying it. The breakfast she spread for him was about the same as yesterday. And every bit as good. He was almost through it, when he heard a clomping of boot heels from somewhere within the house.

He looked up apprehensively as Chuck's voice rang through the halls.

"Amelia!"

"He always holler like that?" he asked her.

She nodded. "He don't mean nothing, Mister Seth. He's a good boy. Please now . . ."

"Sure. I promise. *I* won't start anything."

"He won't neither," she said hopefully.

The boy halted in the doorway and gazed at Seth. He looked like hell. His clothes were sloppily thrown on, his hair uncombed, and his eyes red-rimmed.

Seth gazed back at him, wondering if he were hung over. Damned young for that sort of thing. Or maybe yesterday had been something special. Had the kid primed his courage to go back-shooting?

No, he told himself. Whoever was behind that rifle had been nervous, but not likkered up. Maybe he'd done his drinking later, to console himself for having missed such an easy shot.

The kid's face was sullen and defiant. He looked willing enough to explode. But he didn't. He seemed to be working hard at close-reining himself. Scowling, he started to turn away.

Talk sensible with each other, Seth thought. He asked, "Truce?"

"Damn you," the boy mumbled. He spread his fingers and rubbed his palm on his pants leg, where a gun would have hung if he'd been wearing one.

As he turned his back, Seth called at him, "Hold on a minute."

Halting stiffly on the stairs, Chuck turned again. He eyed Seth narrowly as he snapped, "You leave me be!" Rubbing at his face, he added in a mumble, "Pa said you would."

His shirt sleeves were unbuttoned. When he reached up, the cuff fell back. Seth saw the still-red welt on his arm.

So the old man whipped this one too, he thought. Having J.B. for a father probably wasn't any easier for Chuck than it had been for him. He asked, "Why'd he strap you?"

The boy glared at him. "How'd you know?"

"You think he never laid it onto me?" Seth shot a glance at the welt.

Chuck turned his arm and saw the mark. Jerking the cuff closed, he buttoned it. Darkly, he answered, "On account of you."

"Why?" Seth asked, puzzled.

The kid buttoned the other cuff, then stuck his hands into his pockets and faced Seth. The anger in his voice mixed with shame. "He took my gun away! Said I couldn't have it back till you left here."

"Boy your age don't need a gun," Amelia said.

"My age!" he snapped back at her. Nodding toward Seth, he said, "I'll bet *he* had a gun when he was my age. I'll bet Pa never whipped *him* when he was my age!"

"I had a gun when I was twelve," Seth said. "And he whipped me when I came home—two days ago."

The kid stared at him as if he couldn't quite swallow that. "Why?"

He shrugged. "Why'd he whip you?"

Chuck hesitated. He didn't seem so sullen now—just uncertain and shame-faced. Mumbling, he admitted, "On account of that ruckus the other night by the corral. He said if I'd stay away from you, you'd leave me be. He said if I make any trouble for you while you're here, he'll skin me. And he took my gun away."

It didn't make much sense. But then nothing around here did. The kid looked as if he couldn't figure things out either. Seth leaned his elbows on the table and said, "Come on in and eat. I ain't gonna fight with you."

Still hesitant, Chuck came on down the stairs. But he stopped at the bottom to look thoughtfully at Seth. He asked again, "Why did you come back to JayBar?"

86

"I needed a place to stop for a while. I didn't come here to make trouble for you or your Ma."

Chuck looked as if he couldn't quite believe that either.

Seth rubbed a hand across his face. This kind of talking wasn't easy. But he wanted to make peace with this kid, if he could. He had to try. He added, "I'm not a killer."

"They say you are."

"Who says?"

"They say you're a real fast hand with a gun."

"For a drover maybe," he said. "I keep in practice winning bets for the crew and shooting for drinks. And I don't often lose. But that's *all*."

The kid eyed him askance. "You killed your brother."

"Mister Charles," Amelia interrupted, looking frightened.

Seth struggled to keep his voice level. "That was an accident."

"They say you were too good a hunter to shoot a *man* by mistake."

"*They say!* I guess *they* say Jeremy and I were all the time fighting each other too. *They* say I had plenty of reason to want him dead!"

Chuck nodded.

"Goddammit! You and your damned *they!* Can't . . ."

"Mister Charles," Amelia shouted, cutting Seth short. "You sit down now. Your breakfast is almost ready."

Seth realized his tension. He forced open his clenched fists and eased back into the chair.

Chuck took a step forward and jerked out the chair across the table from him. He dropped into it as if he'd been dared to sit down.

"That's better," Amelia said, almost sighing. "You two *ought* to get along fine together. Don't neither one of you drink milk."

It struck Seth funny. He began to laugh so hard he could barely catch his breath. But it wasn't *that* funny. No—he'd gotten tight-wound, about to explode, only Amelia had stopped him in time. Now, laughing, he could feel the tension ease. He was grateful for her interruption. He glanced at her, and she began to laugh too. Chuck stared from one to the other as if he thought they were both crazy.

Amelia hurried to put a breakfast plate in front of Chuck. Then she poured coffee for Seth. He busied himself with it while he tried to figure out words that would make sense of what he wanted to say. He felt a damned strong urge to square things and reach an understanding with this kid. Somehow that had become very important to him.

When he was sure he could hold his voice steady, he said, "Yeah, Jeremy and I fought each other a lot. Only we got along fine a lot, too. That's what *they* forget. We'd fight and sull a while and then it'd be over. And if anybody tried to haul off on one of us, he had both of us to fight. There were plenty of times when—hell— You couldn't have wanted any better brother than Jeremy. Once we'd get away from this place and Pa, and pack off into the woods to hunt together or something, we'd . . ."

He stopped talking and rubbed at his face, as if he meant to hide behind the hand. The kid was studying him, frowning in puzzlement.

He asked himself what the hell it was that he was trying to say. Dammit, he was no good with words. And words wouldn't explain how it had been between him and Jeremy. But he wanted to make Chuck understand that he hadn't done murder. For God's sake—not to Jeremy!

He told himself to start over again. This time try to make sense without getting all tangled up in feelings.

"Chuck, the way it was with Jeremy and me, if one of us did a thing, the other one did it too. We both got given handguns at the same time. We burnt a hell of a lot of powder trying to outdraw and outshoot each other. But I was always quicker. A damn sight quicker. If I'd *wanted* to kill Jeremy, I could have faced him and done it."

"They say you wouldn't on account of Pa," Chuck told him. This time it didn't sound like an accusation, but just a statement. "They say you made it look like a hunting accident so Pa wouldn't hold you to blame, but that he did anyway."

"Yeah, *he* did," Seth muttered. "The law took my word it was an accident, but Pa wouldn't believe me. What the hell did he want from me?"

As the words slipped out, he had a sudden terrible feeling that he'd bared himself to the bone. He felt naked and unarmed—completely vulnerable. Swallowing back the rising sense of panic, he twisted it into anger: *Laugh at me, damn you, and I'll put your teeth down your gullet!*

"You want some more coffee, Mister Seth?" Amelia said.

He realized he'd half-risen, his fists clenched again. His eyes met hers, and the frightened anger that had flared in him disappeared. He sat back into the chair, bewildered. Without anger, he felt helpless. He glanced furtively at Amelia, as if he expected her to strike out at him.

But she was busy slicing pie. And Chuck was gazing at his own hands as if he were lost in some private thought.

Seth drew breath, trying to loosen the knotted muscles of his shoulders and telling himself he was a damn fool. He was letting JayBar fray at his nerves till he was coming apart.

He muttered, "Hell, it didn't make much difference. I had a pretty mean name around here anyway."

Chuck glanced at him. "Why'd he whip you?"

"For coming back here, I reckon."

"On account of Jeremy?"

"On account of a lot of things."

Amelia set slices of pie in front of them both. As he forked into his, Chuck mumbled, "He don't like me much either." He looked like he'd embarrassed himself with the admission. Quickly he got very busy eating.

Seth took a bite of pie, but he barely tasted it. He was wondering what J.B. asked of this kid. Chuck was all right. Feisty maybe, but plenty game and trying hard. What the hell did the old man want from a son anyway?

Chapter 9

They were still at the table when Seth heard horses. It sounded like two of them on the gravel drive out front, not in harness but under saddle and coming in fast. It sounded like trouble.

Amelia heard them too. She had already started for the door when a rapping of the knocker echoed through the house. Seth rose to follow her, with the kid coming along behind him. He stopped in the doorway of the grand entry.

The room was full two stories high, with a huge crystal chandelier hanging from the ceiling. A wide staircase rose in a curve along the back wall to a landing, there it branched into galleries leading to the upper rooms. As he glanced around, he thought again of the old Southern homes that had been converted to bordellos during the years since the war.

Amelia swung the big front door open. Beyond her, he could see two men on the gallery. He recognized the one who pulled off his hat and started to speak. That was Lamar Glynn from down to Jubilee. The other was a stranger.

Glynn started as he caught sight of Seth. And the other man shoved into the room, grabbing at the gun on his thigh. Leveling it, he shouted, "Hold it there, Yarborough!"

Seth looked from one man to the other. Glynn pushed back the skirt of his coat, showing the butt of the handgun he wore, and the star pinned to his vest.

Lifting his hands away from his sides, Seth said, "Morning, Glynn. You still the law in this county?"

The sheriff nodded, his face expressionless. "Heard you were back, Seth. You know Dave Ludlow here?" He shrugged toward the man with the drawn gun.

Seth shook his head.

"Special deputy from Spence County in Kansas. He's got a warrant for your arrest."

"Is it any good *here?*"

Glynn looked as if he'd just bit into something that he didn't much like the taste of. "You mean on *Yarborough* land?"

"I mean on the Colorado side of the line."

"It's good enough for me to take you in. They've asked for my cooperation."

"He can't just up and haul me back across the state line though, can he?"

"I s'pose you could fight extradition," the sheriff answered. "But the governor'll grant it, Yarborough or not."

"I can stall like hell, can't I?"

"Maybe. What difference would it make?"

"Plenty. Spence County's been aching a long while to hang itself a drover. I got to stay clear of there till I can get square of this business."

Glynn looked like the taste in his mouth had got worse. "You always did figure J.B. could buy you out of anything, didn't you?"

Seth nodded.

"Then you won't make any trouble? You'll come along peaceable?"

"First thing in the morning," Seth answered. "But I got something to tend to this afternoon. You got my parole I'll come in first thing tomorrow."

"Like hell!" the Kansas deputy snapped. He gestured with his gun. "You got no choice, Yarborough."

Seth looked to Glynn questioningly.

"*Murder* warrant," the sheriff said. "In case you don't know it, murder is a serious business. I can't take your parole on a thing like this."

Seth heard the boy behind him draw breath in surprise and grunt, "Murder!"

Dammit, in that one word, he'd lost all the ground he'd won toward making peace with the kid. And what he had in mind now was just going to make it worse. But it was the only way. Nothing else was as important as seeing Annie Johnson.

He judged that the kid was plenty close enough, peering over his shoulder that way. And that damned lawman didn't show any sign of cooperating. With a shrug, he drawled, "Well now, Glynn, I 'spose . . ."

Wheeling suddenly, he grabbed Chuck, his arm wrapping around the boy's neck. As he swung the kid in front of him, his other hand was bringing up the Colt. Under the boy's arm, he leveled it toward the Kansas lawman. "Drop it, Mister!"

Ludlow let his gun slide out of his fingers and raised both hands, cursing under his breath. His face was turning a dull brick-red.

Seth looked toward Glynn. But the sheriff didn't move. His voice firm, he said, "If you run now, J.B. won't be able to help you. You'll just be making it worse for yourself."

"I give you my parole."

"If you really think you can clear yourself in Kansas, you'd better give me that gun and come on along peaceably." The sheriff held a hand tentatively toward him.

He shook his head. "I can't do a damn thing for myself *in* Kansas. Not with the kind of lynch mobs they got. But I don't mind setting around *your* jail a while. . . ."

"Then . . ."

"Only I got something to tend to first, Glynn. I can't come with you right now."

Glynn eyed the gun. "Dammit, Seth, you ain't gonna shoot."

The kid was struggling against Seth's grip. Tightening his arm, he mumbled, "Hold it, Chuck. Easy." But it didn't do any good. The boy kept twisting, fighting to break free. Dammit, wasn't anybody ever going to believe anything he said?

Seth looked at the sheriff and grinned. It was a cold, almost vicious grin. "Either you *can* trust me and you've got my parole. Or else you *can't* trust me and I'm liable to start putting holes in you. Take your choice, Glynn."

Slowly, with a deep reluctant sigh, the sheriff raised his hands.

Seth glanced at Amelia. She was standing wide-eyed, staring at him with confused disapproval. He asked, "You know anything about guns?"

"A little bit."

"You take theirs and empty the loads out."

"Mister Seth, I don't think . . ."

"Please, Amelia."

She moved slowly, picking up the gun Ludlow had dropped, then taking Glynn's from his holster. With fumbling hands, she poked out the cartridges. When she was done, she held the handful of them toward Seth.

"Throw 'em on the floor."

She put them down in a neat heap. As she moved away, he gave them a kick that scattered them across the room. Then, his grip still strong on Chuck, he sidestepped, forcing the boy to move with him. He hated doing it this way but . . . He wondered if he'd ever be able to explain, ever get the chance. He edged toward the door. As his shoulders touched it, he loosened his grip slightly.

"You damned liar!" Chuck gasped at him.

"Hold off on me," he mumbled. "Ain't got time now. Talk later."

Suddenly—shoving the boy away from him—he jerked open the door and wheeled through it. Slamming it shut, he ran toward the horses.

They stood at the hitching post, alert at his appearance. The grulla looked the better animal. He grabbed loose both sets of reins and flung himself onto the grulla's saddle—a sharp slap of the reins at the other horse's rump, at the same time ramming his spurs into the grulla's flanks and both horses jumped. He let the other one run loose. His attention was on the grulla that lunged, stretching out, moving fast and striding long. Bent low over the fork, he was turning it onto the road toward the cover of a stand of trees when he heard Glynn's shout of warning.

The shot that followed was a warning, too. It went too wide to have been aimed at him. And before Glynn could fire again, he was past that stand of fir, out of sight of the house.

He figured it wouldn't take the lawmen long to get a couple of JayBar horses saddled and follow on his trail. Staying to the road at a full run, he gained distance. Reaching the water ford, he turned sharply, reining downstream. Then he scrambled the horse up the bank, making sure that its hooves left only faint traces in the grass. Onto a broad swathe of rock, then across it and, using his spurs, he jumped the grulla back into the water. At a hard run again, he headed upstream. Let 'em hunt that trail a while.

He was well out of sight of the road, halted to let the grulla breathe, when he heard the drum of hooves, faint in the distance. He could hear them stop at the ford. They'd expect him to turn there and they'd be searching for his sign. They'd find it downstream. But nowhere else. Not unless they hunted close for a hell of a long time and had a damned lot of luck with them. These mountains were *his*—at least as far as knowing the ways through them. It was a game he and Jeremy had played as boys. They'd tracked each other over the rocks and through the forests and streams until they knew the ground and the ways of crossing it without leaving sign.

He gigged the grulla lightly and moved on at an amble. Well out of earshot of the road, he picked up to a lope. When he came onto the park, it was from above. Annie was already there, dismounted and letting her horse graze while she waited for him.

She smiled when he appeared out of the forest, trotting toward her. But then the smile faded. Her eyes were wide with question. "Seth! That's Lamar Glynn's horse!"

He nodded as he drew rein. "Likely he's looking for it right now. Mount up and ride a ways with me, Annie. I've got to talk to you."

Catching the sorrel's reins, she stepped up to her saddle. As she moved to his side, she asked, "Are you in trouble?"

That came damn near being funny. He said, "When ain't I been?"

Her face was very solemn. "Serious trouble?"

"I'm going in come morning. I'll be arrested when I do. I wanted to see you first though. I wanted to tell you about it myself."

"Tell me what?"

"I got into some trouble in Kansas. That's why I came back to JayBar. Only now this deputy's showed up. I guess he followed my trail . . ."

"But why, Seth?"

He realized he was stalling, trying to figure out just how to say it to her. But there was only one right way—the truth, straight out. "He's got a murder warrant on me."

"No! Not murder!"

For a moment he was sorry he'd come, sorry he'd told her. Her face had gone pale, shocked, as if he'd hit her.

"It wasn't murder when it happened," he mumbled. He'd run out of words, run out of ways to explain himself. How the hell do you explain just how you'd happened to kill a man? How do you explain it when this is the second time it's happened to you?

Quietly, Annie said, "Tell me about it."

"I'm a drover." That was a part of it, he thought. That was the beginning. Reining the grulla into a stream, he gestured for her to follow. She rode silently behind him, the horses' hooves splashing in the water, seeming uncommon loud.

When the stream widened, he motioned for her to come up alongside. She looked at him, her eyes asking for the rest of it.

"A shooting scrape," he told her. "We had the herd on the bed-grounds near to Horseshoe and a bunch of us went into town. Got drunk and rowdy, I guess." He paused, thinking that didn't sound much in his favor. Drawing a deep breath, he plunged himself into it, telling it the way it had been. "One of the drovers got into an argument with a bartender in the saloon. It turned into a fight and the next thing I knew the sonofa—the bartender—had a gun in his hand and was beating my pal in the face with it. Looked to me like he meant to bust his head open with it. I hollered at him and drew. He snapped a shot at me and I fired back. Only my aim was better than his."

"You killed him?"

He nodded. That was it, the whole of it. He asked, "You want me to take you home now?"

"But that wasn't *murder*," she protested. "Not if he was shooting at you!"

She'd listened and she'd believed him. "It wasn't then," he said. "Everybody who saw it agreed to that. But everybody who saw it was drovers."

"Does that make a difference?"

"In Horseshoe it does. Drovers were welcome enough there at first. The town was built with cattle money. Drovers'd spend their wages and the town was getting rich. But now it's settled and full of *respectable* folk who got no use for trail hands in their town. They'll sell us their goods at damned high prices and take our money in pay for 'em, but they don't want us hanging around in their town. To them, it ain't the killing that counts. It's me being a drover and him being a resident of their fair city. Hell, he wouldn't have been there but to profit by selling drinks to drovers. . . ."

"But the *law*, Seth!"

"People make the law the way they want it," he answered her. "They write a law and then they call whatever happens by a name that'll make it fit the law. Me killing him wasn't murder when it happened. But that night a bunch of those *respectable* folk showed up at our camp with guns. The trail boss met 'em and talked to 'em. They claimed they were deputies and said they wanted me. Looked a damn sight more like vigilantes."

"What happened?"

"Boss and the boys ran 'em off. He gave me a good horse and told me I'd better get to hell up the back trails till I was a long ways out of that county." He glanced over his shoulder. "Guess I didn't go far enough."

Her eyes were wide and uncertain. "They mean to hang you?"

He shook his head. "Not if I can stall long enough. Pa's sent a man to Horseshoe. He'll get me out of it somehow. The kind of law they got there, if it gets busted money'll mend it."

"It's not right."

He wasn't sure whether she meant the way the law worked, or the way he was trying to fight it. He mumbled, "Damned lot of things ain't right. A man has to get by the best he can. It wasn't murder and I'll get out of hanging for it any way I can."

When she didn't say anything, he faced her and asked, "Do you fault me for that?"

"No."

"Well, I've told you the *truth* of it. If Glynn locks me up, likely you'll hear worse."

"If I do, I won't believe it." She was smiling at him, a small worried smile that was obviously meant to be reassuring.

He grinned at her, a little awed that she'd believe him —and worry about him, too. "Annie, will you ride up to the pool with me again? Might be this is the last chance I'll have to see you for a while."

Nodding, she said, "You promised to take me to the dance at Tatums' a week from Saturday."

"Could be a mite difficult, if Glynn locks me up. I don't know how long this business'll take."

"If he does, I'll bake you a pie with a file in it," she said firmly.

By the time they reached the pool and dismounted at the water's edge, Glynn and the warrant, all the trouble, seemed far away and unimportant. The only thing that mattered to Seth right then was the moment and the girl.

She continued to amaze him. She had brought lunch—a real spread of food, even a tablecloth, stuffed into her saddle pockets. As she set it all out, she explained, "I wanted you to have a chance to sample my cooking."

She didn't meet his eyes as she said it, and he could see the traces of color on her cheeks. He wondered if she really meant it the way it sounded. He kept thinking about it as they ate and talked. The conversation was all light and trivial, and all through it his mind worked at other thoughts about her.

It had been a hell of a long time since he'd considered the possibility of some day settling to a home and family. He'd wiped that idea out of his future six years ago. But now it was back, stronger and more appealing than ever it had been in those wild days.

When they were done eating she cleared up and put away the tablecloth. While she did that, he leaned back in the sun. Content and drowsy, he closed his eyes against its brightness, feeling the warmth of it on his face. It was good—being here with her—it should go on like this forever. He wondered if it could. Was there any way he could wrench the world around, upend it, twist it and shake it, and come out on top for a change?

"Are you going to sleep?" he heard her ask in that half-smiling, teasing voice.

"Yeah," he mumbled.

She must have scooped up both hands full of water. It splashed cold and sudden into his face. He sat up with a start, blinking his eyes open, and she shook her wet fingers at him.

He lunged, grabbing at her. Wrapping his hands around her wrists, he pulled her down. For a moment they struggled, mock-wrestling, both laughing. He was on his back in the grass, with her weight across his chest, and her face close to his. And suddenly, he wasn't laughing. He was pulling her head down, finding her mouth with his.

She was motionless, yielding, but not returning the kiss. And then she was pulling out of his arms to rise to her feet.

Abashed, he sat up, meaning to apologize somehow. He hoped to hell she'd forgive him. What kind of damn fool was he to do a thing like that?

But she was smiling. Her voice teasing again, she said,

"You swore a solemn and horrible oath, Seth Yarborough. You'll burn in Hades."

"Be worth it," he said and grinned, reaching for her hand.

She drew back and the smile was gone. "No, Seth, please . . ."

"Annie, I want to marry you," he said. He surprised himself. He'd been thinking about it, but he sure hadn't meant to speak about it. Not yet. Not until he had a lot of things worked out. A hell of a lot of things.

She turned away from him and gazed down into the pool.

It had been wrong to say it now, he thought. Always saying the wrong damned thing at the wrong damned time. But it was said. Now, he had to make her understand.

"That's what I'm asking, Annie. It's all I'm asking. You don't have to answer me now. I won't even ask now. But afterward, once I've got everything straightened out, then I'll ask you."

She didn't move. He couldn't see her face. He wanted desperately to know what she was thinking. Glancing at his faded britches, he said, "I know I don't look like much now, but I ain't tried for much. I've been working for found and drinking money. If I put myself to it, I can do better though. Might be I couldn't keep you the way that your folks do, but I can keep a roof over your head and food on the table. . . ."

She turned toward him. Her eyes were shining as if they were damp with tears. But she was smiling. "And I can make my clothes out of feed sacks and take in laundry! It sounds wonderful! Don't wait, Seth, ask me now!"

She meant it, he thought, amazed. "You will marry me? You'll come with me, away from here?"

"I'll go anywhere with you, Seth. If you ask me, I'll go trail herding with you."

"I'd ask"—he grinned—"only I don't think the boss would much cotton to the idea."

"We could run away together. Now."

He wanted to. But too many things were too wrong now. That would just make it all worse. He told her, "I've got to get clear of this trouble I'm in. And I ought to talk to your folks. I don't want to run off with you like a thief. Do you think your father would listen to *me?*"

She nodded. But the doubts were pushing in on him

again, crowding him, forcing him back into a corner. He muttered, "I've got a pretty mean name around here."

"If he says no, we'll run away," she said, chanting lightly. He recognized it for a line from an old song. But he was damned serious.

"I've done enough running. I don't like it. Might be best if I got set somewhere first. Got some money and a place to take you before I ask him."

She shook her head firmly. Bending, she brushed his cheek with her lips, then whispered, "I'll go with you—now."

The doubts were faded, unimportant. He grinned again. "You figure you've got me roped, tied, marked and branded?"

"Yes!"

"You're right. Come 'ere." He wrapped his hand around her wrist and pulled her toward him. He held her, and this time she returned his kiss. And he knew it was right. All the rest—all the troubles—could be worked out somehow. This was what was important. This was *right*.

Chapter 10

The Johnson place was a white-painted cottage set on a slope a bit away from the edge of the woods, with a small meadow stretching out in front of it. As they reached the ridge overlooking it, Annie started to draw rein. But Seth shook his head. He'd already made his decision: In trouble or out of it, he was still Seth Yarborough. And he had to know what he was up against here.

"I'm riding on in with you, Annie," he said.

"Now?"

"I got to face your father sometime. Be better if I do it now. It'll give him a fair chance to argue you out of this."

"He couldn't argue me out of it with a shotgun," she answered. Edging the sorrel until it almost rubbed flanks with his bay, she reached out. He wrapped his hand over hers and leaned from the saddle to kiss her lightly.

Holding the horses close together, they rode on toward the house. And as they neared the front gallery, the door opened.

"Annie, you're late. I was beginning to . . ." The man who stepped onto the gallery started as he saw the rider at her side. "Who's this?"

For an instant Seth felt the doubts. This was the wrong time, he thought. He should have waited. . . .

"It's Seth Yarborough," she answered her father.

He repeated the name as if he didn't quite believe it and leaned forward slightly to peer at Seth in the lowering twilight.

Feeling damned uncomfortable under his scrutiny, Seth stepped off the horse and offered Annie a hand down. He clung to her hand a moment, then released it and followed her up the steps.

Johnson stepped back from the doorway. Blank-voiced, he said, "Come on in."

Seth pulled off his hat as he followed Annie into the house. The lamps were lit and he glanced curiously around the living room at the low-raftered ceiling, the painted walls and curtained windows. There was a big stone fireplace, an upholstered sofa and rawhide-bottomed chairs, and a parlor organ with a whale-oil lamp on it. Bright-colored hooked rugs were scattered on the floor and there were framed pictures on the walls. It was a warm, friendly room. This was the way he'd want his own house to be, he thought.

He asked Annie, "Do you play the organ?"

She nodded.

"Annie, your mother's in the kitchen," Johnson said. "Go tell her you're home safe, will you?"

With a quick smile toward Seth, she left the room. He watched the door swing closed behind her, then turned toward her father.

Johnson was a fairly tall man, thickening at the waist and thinning at the hairline. His eyes were about the same shade of blue as Annie's. They seemed clouded over as he studied Seth. In a dark and meaningful voice, he said, "Lamar Glynn was around here a while ago with some Kansan. I suppose you know why."

Seth nodded. That was a rotten piece of luck. He'd hoped that if he told Johnson himself he could make the man understand. But now Johnson had heard it from Glynn, and probably thought the worst.

"I hope to hell you've got a good story, Yarborough. For Annie's sake. I know my daughter and . . ."

"You know?"

"Once I heard you were back in these parts, I was pretty sure where she'd been riding off to in the afternoons. She's a stubborn, willful girl. God knows she's had callers aplenty these past few years. Some of 'em I thought she might really care about. Always ended up the same though, with her sending them away and then riding out, hanging around JayBar range. Once she gets her mind set on a thing . . ."

"Father!" Annie had stepped back into the living room. She scowled at him. "What on earth are you telling Seth?"

"The truth. He's entitled to know." He scowled back at

her. "And I expect the same from him. You know he's wanted for murder?"

She nodded. "He told me."

"Look, Mister Johnson," Seth began. "It's kind of a mess. . . ."

"I don't doubt that."

"But I figure I can get it straightened out. I'm going down to see Glynn in the morning. I . . ." He paused, not sure what to say next. Annie moved to his side, taking his hand in hers. He looked at her. "Maybe you'd better tell him. If I try, I'll say something wrong for sure."

Johnson listened his daughter out as she repeated the story Seth had told her. With a weary shake of his head, he walked to the sideboard and pulled out a bottle and two glasses.

Handing one drink to Seth, he muttered, "I can't say I like it. Can't say I like it at all. I hope to hell this is the truth, Yarborough."

"I swear it," Seth answered. Bending toward Annie, he whispered, "A solemn and horrible oath."

"What?" Johnson frowned.

Annie laughed. She prodded Seth in the ribs as she told her father, "It *is* the truth. I know it is."

Johnson swallowed down his drink, then stared into the empty glass as if he couldn't decide whether or not to fill it up again. Finally, he set it down. "I *could* object," he said thoughtfully. "I could turn you over to the law myself and hope they hang you. But it wouldn't do me any good. Once this girl's made up her mind, there's no holding her. I could tie her up, but she'd get loose. She'd follow you straight to the gallows. . . ."

"Father!"

"He's got as much right to know what he's getting into as you have," he snapped back at her. Then he looked at Seth. "This is *her* idea, you know. She's had her cap set for you for years."

Seth wiped a hand self-consciously across his face. He'd had more than a hint of that from Annie. He mumbled, "I don't understand it, but I'm damned glad of it."

Annie poked him in the ribs again. "You!"

"Can't say *I* understand it either," her father added. "But once she's made up her mind—always the women who decide these things, you know. They let us think it's our own idea, but it's always theirs. The way her mother and I— Well, that's none of your business. But if you hadn't come back, I think before long she'd have packed out looking for you. . . ."

"Father!" Annie's face was a bright red now.

Seth grinned at her. Turning to Johnson, he said, "It's what I want, too."

"Well, you won't have any blessing from me. Not until you've cleared up this murder charge."

"Then?"

"Then you take your time and court my daughter proper. Stop this sneaking around in the woods. You willing to do that? Willing to prove you can make a decent home for her?"

Seth nodded.

Glancing toward the kitchen door, Johnson called, "Ma, come on out here and say hello to Seth Yarborough."

The woman who hurried through the doorway was slight, not as tall as Annie, but with the same shape to her face and the same kind of warm smile. She wiped her hands on her apron as she looked Seth over.

Johnson started, "Ma, we've been talking about . . ."

"I know. I've been listening at the door." She had the same kind of teasing voice as Annie, too. "So you're the Yarborough boy. You've certainly changed since the last time I saw you. I hope you've got a decent suit. I wouldn't want my Annie standing up with you dressed like that."

"No ma'am," he said. "But I'll get me one."

She looked him down again, critically, as if she were picturing him properly dressed. Nodding with satisfaction, she said, "Will you stay for supper, Mister Yarborough?"

The sheriff's office wasn't open yet when Seth reached town. He'd slept the night in Johnson's barn and then ridden directly to Jubilee. With his gunbelt looped over his shoulder, he sat perched on the hitch rail in front of the office, idly watching a shopkeeper across the street sweep the walk.

It was early, still quiet, with the shadows stretched out long and thin, when he spotted Lamar Glynn ambling down the street. Glynn eyed him expressionlessly.

"Morning," Seth said, touching his hat brim to the sheriff. The gesture came out more insolent than polite.

Glynn nodded slightly and searched a key out of his pocket. Seth slipped the gunbelt down his arm and held it out, but the sheriff ignored it as he opened the door. Seth walked in, glanced around and slung the belt over one of the wall pegs. Shoving his hat onto the back of his head, he said, "I left your horse at the stable. Real fine animal."

Glynn faced him then. "You're pretty damned sure of yourself, ain't you?"

Seth shrugged. "Why not?"

"Someday you'll get yourself into something that money can't buy you out of." Glynn motioned toward the back room. Seth followed the gesture and walked into the room. There were two cells, both empty.

"Not much business," he said.

"More than enough for me," the sheriff answered. He slammed the barred door shut behind Seth and turned his key in the lock.

Seth looked at the small bar-crossed window, then at the closed door, feeling an edge of panic. What if *this* was the time—what if J.B.'s money couldn't buy him out of a hanging? What the hell was he doing to himself, surrendering this way?

He jammed his hands down into his pockets and eyed the sheriff. "How long you reckon this business is gonna take?"

"Why?" Glynn snapped. "You're not *worried,* are you?"

Seth stopped himself from a sharp answer. Instead, he grunted, "I got better things to do than loaf around here."

Glynn stood there, studying him, and under that gaze he began to feel damned uncomfortable. He sat down on the cot and put his hands to making a smoke. He'd got it built and lit and Glynn still hadn't moved. Finally, he demanded, "What the hell are you staring at?"

"Trouble on the hoof. Why don't you do one decent thing for a change and get the hell out of that old man's life?"

"Huh?"

"He's pulled you out of the fire often enough already. If he manages it again, why don't you get? Go away from here and leave him alone. He's got enough troubles without you bringing him more."

Seth took a long drag on the cigarette. When he met Glynn's eyes, he said quietly. "That's just exactly what I'm planning to do, Sheriff."

For an instant there was expression in the sheriff's face

—a flash of surprise as sudden as summer lightning. Then it was gone. "We thought he was rid of you six years ago," he said. "But now you've come runnnig back. You'll be back again next time you need him."

"Did J.B. buy you that tin star?" Seth snapped. "He tell you to run me out of town when this business is cleared up?"

Glynn shook his head. "You think money can buy everything?"

"J.B.'s money can."

"Someday you're going to find out different, Yarborough. Some day you're going to stick your neck out too damned far, and you're going to get your head lopped off."

Before Seth could answer back, the sheriff had wheeled and stalked out. Angrily, Seth stubbed out the cigarette and leaned his back against the wall. What the hell did Glynn want of him? He'd given his parole and he'd come in. He'd let himself be locked up. Did he have to take Glynn's tongue lashing, too? Glancing at the locked door, he told himself he guessed he did. He'd got himself into a spot where he couldn't walk out or fight back, either one.

The morning dragged by with a damned intolerable slowness. And then Annie Johnson came visiting. With a pie. At her insistence, Glynn left them alone together, with the barred door between them.

As Seth forked into the pie, he almost expected to hit the hard lump of a file. When he didn't, Annie explained, "This one's just for practice. I'll bake the file in next time."

They laughed together, and talked, mostly making plans. She seemed disappointed when he told her he intended to go droving again.

"To get a stake," he said. "I've got to get myself enough money to buy a suit."

"There's a lot of cattle work around here. Couldn't you get a ranch job within riding distance?"

He shook his head. "J.B. wouldn't cotton to it."

"What's he got to do with it?" she asked.

"For one thing, I think he's already told Glynn to run me out of the county."

"He can't order the sheriff around that way."

He didn't want to argue with her. Instead, he said, "For another thing, the cattlemen around here all belong to the

Association. If one of them was to hire me on, J.B. would pressure him out of it quick enough."

"J.B. can't order the Association around that way either," she protested.

"Can't he? He owns this whole county, and you know it."

"He owns JayBar and some business interests. That's *all* he owns. The people run the county. *They* elected Sheriff Glynn. Why, J.B. isn't even president of the Association any more."

"Huh?" That was a surprising bit of news.

"Gil Nash has been president for the last two years," she told him. "J.B. is just a member, like everyone else. Like my father."

He shook his head. "Maybe it *looks* that way. But I know J.B."

"Do you, Seth?" she said sincerely.

"I damned well should. He raised me. He's whipped me and shoved me and . . . hell, I know the old man. He runs Long County. Maybe he runs the whole damned state now. I hear he's real cozy with the governor."

"My father has a standing invitation to dinner with the governor any time he's in Denver," she answered firmly. "That doesn't mean my father runs the state of Colorado."

"Your father isn't J.B. Yarborough. Mine is."

"Seth, even if he could, I don't think J.B. would *want* to run the state, or the county, or anything bigger than JayBar. And I'm not even sure he wants to keep running that."

He snorted skeptically.

"J.B. is getting old and he knows it," she continued. "A lot of people think he married the widow O'Connor because of her son. Because he wanted to bring the boy along to take over JayBar in a few years. Then he can set back and rest, let the boy handle the reins."

"You know him real well, don't you?"

"Better than you think. Don't forget, my father *is* a member of the Association. We attend socials at JayBar. I've seen J.B. during the years you've been away. He's getting old, Seth, and he's tired. He may have been a hard-driving man once, but I think he just wants to rest now."

"He's *never* going to give up being king of the hill," Seth said. "It's all he ever cared about."

"He loved his family. He cared a lot about Jeremy . . ." She stopped short as she realized what she was saying. It sounded like a lame afterthought when she added, "And you."

"Sure!" he snapped. "He gave me the best horse on the place when he ran me out!"

"Seth," she said softly, "have you tried talking to him about . . .?"

"Goddammit, woman!" He snatched at the growing anger, trying to fight it back. It wasn't Annie's fault. She just didn't know or understand. Shamedly, he wiped at his face, then looked at her again. "You know what you'll be getting into by marrying me? I'm short-fused and ornery. Downright mean."

She nodded. And her mouth hinted that teasing smile again. "Do you plan to beat me?"

He grinned at her, marveling at the way she had about her. She'd get along all right, he thought. She could handle him; she'd be able to hold rein on him a damn sight better than he could himself. He answered her, "Whup you twice a day, extra on Sundays and holidays."

"I'll hit back."

"I reckon you will."

They went on then to talk about other things, the happy things. And when she left, he was feeling real fine, looking forward to her coming back again. But then Lamar Glynn walked in and ruined his mood.

Standing there on the other side of the bars, Glynn looked critical and a little smug as he said, "No bail."

"Huh?" Seth grunted, not sure he'd heard right.

"Judge won't allow you bail. There's some things the Yarborough money won't buy you."

What the devil was Glynn talking about, he wondered. He snapped back, "Did I ask for bail?"

"J.B. drove in to see the judge first thing this morning," the sheriff said. "Didn't you know?"

Puzzled, Seth shook his head. Why would the old man do that?

The sheriff was frowning. "You mean to tell me when you came in this morning, you didn't figure you'd be out on bail by nightfall?"

"I got no money. And I figure J.B.'d bail me out about as quick as he'd put his hand down a hole to feel for a rattler."

"But you *do* plan on him buying back that murder warrant?"

"Yeah, for the sake of the family name. Wouldn't look good having me hanged under the name of Yarborough. Can't see where it'd make any difference to him whether I wait it out in jail or not though," Seth muttered, speaking to himself as much as to the sheriff.

"If you didn't figure to get right back out again, what'd you come in for?" Glynn asked suspiciously.

"I gave you my parole," Seth said. He wondered what he was trying to explain for. "What the hell difference does it make? You got me, ain't you?"

Glynn nodded. Sounding vague, he said, "It might make a lot of difference."

"What's that supposed to mean?"

"J.B. is pretty highly thought of in these parts. So is Annie Johnson. If you've got a streak of decency as wide as a skunk's stripe . . ."

"I'm going to marry Annie Johnson." Seth's voice was hard, cutting knife-sharp across Glynn's words.

"You? Marry her?"

Tight-reined, he said, "Her folks are agreeable to me courting her."

"Maybe they don't know you like I do. Maybe they never seen you turn a peaceable conversation into a blood-fight the way I have."

Silently, Seth cursed the bars that kept the sheriff beyond the throw of his fist.

And as if he could read the thought, Glynn said, "You'd be laying into me right now if you could, wouldn't you?"

Seth struggled to keep his voice calm. "You're not worth the trouble, Sheriff."

"What are you so damned scared of, Yarborough?"

"What the hell makes you think I'm scared of something?"

"You're too quick to bust loose and hit. It's like you think you've got to stop something before it can happen," Glynn answered him. "You're not just proddy. You're spooky. You're like a sore-backed bronc bucking at the *sight* of a saddle."

There was no way to fight back—no way to stop the sheriff's words with his fist—shove them back down his damned throat. Seth's anger was turning back on itself, twisting into a sense of panicked helplessness.

"Goddammit!" he shouted. "What the hell do you want? Can't you leave me be?"

Glynn hesitated, looking as if he were holding a load of words on his tongue, deciding whether to swallow them or spit them out. Unspeaking, he turned and walked away.

Seth glanced around the cell, feeling a desperate need to smash something. He closed his hands on the bars, on the cold, solid iron that held him from fighting back. There was no yield in them. He forced open his fingers and flexed his hands.

Wearily, he dropped onto the cot and sprawled out, pressing his face into the crook of his arm. What the hell did they want from him anyway? he asked himself. And slowly, with the steady persistence of a grindstone, Glynn's question worked its way back into his mind—what was he so damned scared of?

Chapter 11

Annie came to visit him in the afternoons, and while she was there the time went by at a full run. But while she was away it seemed to stand stock still. Seth ate, he slept and he thought. There was nothing else to do. He decided that a man penned with his own thoughts that way could go crazy quickly, and he began to wonder how long it would take.

Four days seemed like that many years—like more. He felt as if he'd been waiting in the damned cell for at least half his lifetime. The fifth day crept slowly along until Annie came. And when she had gone, it dropped back to that slow crawl.

He was lying on the cot with his eyes closed, wishing he could fall asleep, when the sheriff came into the back room. He'd learned the sound of Glynn's steps, and didn't bother to acknowledge his presence.

"Got a telegram." The sheriff's voice was dull, a little disappointed.

Seth blinked and looked at him. "Telegram?"

Glynn nodded. He twisted the key in the lock and jerked the barred door open. "Warrant against you has been dropped. You're free to go."

"About time," Seth grunted as he sat up. He felt the sense of relief. But there was no feeling of pleasure. Instead, he was—hell—he felt almost *disappointed*. Puzzled by his own reaction, he followed Glynn into the office.

His gunbelt was still on the peg where he'd hung it. As he reached for it, the sheriff said to him, "You figure J.B.'s money will buy you any damned thing you want, don't you?"

That was Glynn's tune, and he'd fiddled it before. Seth was beginning to feel sick of hearing it. He started to turn, to snap angrily at the sheriff. But suddenly he understood his own sense of disappointment. The power of that money had just been proven again. J.B. was still king of the hill. He could buy a man's neck out of a noose.

Holding his hand slow, moving with an air of lazy insolence, he lifted down the gunbelt and slung it around his waist. Then he looked toward Glynn and grunted, "Yeah."

"You're wrong," the sheriff said, watching his hands as he drew out and checked the gun. "There might be places where it'll help you out of trouble, but there's a hell of a lot of land where it won't. If you try to stay here—if you make trouble in Long County—you'll hang for it. You keep that in mind, Yarborough."

"I don't intend to make trouble in Long County. I don't intend to *be* in Long County. And stop calling me *Yarborough!*"

The sheriff gazed at him with a questioning frown as he slammed the gun into the holster and wheeled to stalk into the street.

Why had he said *that*, he wondered. He stepped to the edge of the plank walk and looked into the distance at the peak of Bloodyhead Mountain. *Yarborough* was just a name. Maybe not his by right, but the best he had. A man needed some kind of a handle. It would serve as well as any. Why resent being called by it?

Between here and that high peak, the Yarborough mansion sat, presiding over JayBar. He couldn't see the house from here. It was a far ways. But it seemed as if he could feel its chill shadow.

All that fine and fancy talk of Glynn's about the law in Long County didn't prove a damned thing. It was what *happened*, not what men *said*, that counted. Hell of a thing when the right or wrong of what he'd done didn't matter—when it was money—just money, and not justice —that controlled the law. Hell of a thing when J.B. could buy him out of a scrape that the truth couldn't save him from. But what was the truth anyway—just whatever people wanted to believe.

He asked himself if he'd have been willing to hang just to prove that J.B. couldn't master everything he touched. It seemed like a damn fool question. But he couldn't be sure of the answer.

The trip back to JayBar from town was a long one and it was one he didn't fancy making. He didn't want to see that damned monstrosity of a house again—or any of the

111

people in it. He could say to hell with the horse he'd left there, get on a train out of Jubilee. Go back to Texas and find a job, start building a stake. But if he left now, he'd never know whether it had been J.B. shooting at him that day.

And he had a feeling he'd never be able to escape the shadow of JayBar until he had that question answered. It would chafe at him for the rest of his life.

He stood gazing at the distant mountain, thinking it was a lodestone dragging him back to hell. But there was no fighting it. Slowly, reluctantly, he began to walk toward it.

He managed to hitch a ride on a wagon most of the way up the road, but the rest of the distance to the ranch house was a long hard walk. By the time he raised it, the moon was well up into the night sky.

He stopped on the gravel drive to look at the lone window that showed lamplight. So J.B. was sitting up in his study again? Sorrowing over the cost of saving the family name? A bullet in the back would have been a lot cheaper, he thought. What was it Mace had said: *Might be he's decided he owes you more'n he gave you.*

Why couldn't he face the old man and demand an answer from him? What the hell kept him back from voicing the accusation? What was he afraid of?

He started toward the lit window. But then he stopped, knowing he couldn't do it now. Maybe he *was* afraid. He couldn't be sure. But he knew he was too damned weary now to bear up under the kind of scene he'd be getting into. After a night's sleep he'd be able to think more clearly, better able to hold his own against J.B. He could see the old man tomorrow and have it out then. But not now.

As he walked into the yard, he wondered how Mace would react. Probably ask a lot of questions. Well, he had an excuse for coming back to the ranch—had to collect his horse, didn't he?

The bunkhouse was dark. So was the foreman's room. Mace would have turned in hours ago. Let him sleep, Seth thought. He sure didn't feel like talking to anybody right now. He could bed in the barn tonight—face the world tomorrow.

The barn door was open a crack. He was glad of it. He could slip through without creaking the door on its hinges and maybe waking someone by the noise.

As he stepped in, he looked up. The loft door was wide open, spilling a square of thin moonlight onto the barn floor. But the shadows were blacker than pitch. He squinted into them, remembering that there'd been an old saddle blanket hung over the rails of one of the stalls. He could wrap himself in that and bed in the hay.

Groping, he located the blanket by touch. And his shin hit something. A shovel that had been leaning against the rails toppled with a harsh clatter, shattering the stillness.

He froze, breath held, listening. But there were no answering sounds from outside. Looked as if nobody'd wakened to the noise. Sighing, he slung the blanket over his shoulder and started up the ladder to the loft.

He sensed the presence as he reached the top rung. In the same instant that he realized he wasn't alone here, something cracked him in the face.

It rammed out from above—something like a sharp-heeled boot—slamming a tine of pain through his face. As it rocked his head back, he felt his fingers slipping off the ladder.

He fell hard, sprawling with the breath knocked out of him. And whoever had kicked him was scrambling down the ladder to try again.

Rolling, he grabbed at the boot that brushed his ribs. He couldn't see the attacker here in the dark shadows, but he could hear heavily drawn breath. And he could smell the mixed man and horse odors, sense the warmth of the body so close to him. He grabbed out and caught the boot. Jerking, he brought the man down.

The boot wrenched out of his hands. He scrambled to his feet, knowing the attacker did the same. Crouching, he tried to sense the man's position. His face hurt like hell. He brushed the back of his hand against his cheek. Didn't feel like there was any bleeding.

The attacker was suddenly kicking at him again. The boot scraped his knee, almost tripping him. He felt his shoulder brush a post and grabbed at it for support. He could sense the bulk of the man who was after him. A big man—fast-moving for the size of him—an angry man, lunging toward him, meaning to grapple.

He sidestepped, swinging into the darkness. His fist landed—hard belly muscle under his knuckles and a sharp grunt of pain. A fist that felt like a sledge hammer rammed

113

against the side of his neck. He swung again—into a shoulder?

He tried to judge the man's position in the darkness. Hands were grabbing for him. He ducked and a hard-driven, evil-intentioned knee brushed his thigh. Wheeling, he bent low behind the post, aware of the attacker's groping hunt for him.

The man would be sensing and scenting him, too. He kept his head low, knowing that those big, hard hands were outstretched, searching the darkness for him. He moved in under one, driving with both fists knotted, ramming them with all his weight behind them.

He struck belly muscle again. And felt the flex of bottom ribs under his blow. The attacker reeled back, grasping for breath—but not going down. A damned hard man.

Twisting his body, he sidestepped as the attacker caught balance and lunged. He wouldn't stand a chance if that grizzly got a hug on him. This was like fighting Jeremy—he had to depend on his quickness against his opponent's strength. But Jeremy had never sought him with the kind of vicious determination he sensed in this enemy.

He wheeled, both hands fisted together again, arms outstretched. That swing slammed the big man in the back, just above the hip. And Seth flung himself away as the man spun to strike back. Knuckles like rock brushed his shoulder.

Crouching low, he took another step back into the darkness, away from the big man. Something flickered at the corner of his eye. He glanced toward it. There on the edge of the loft, he saw a figure. It was skylit against the open loading door.

The woman was kneeling, peering down toward the fight, her long hair loose on her shoulders. He couldn't see her face, but he didn't need to. Startled, he stared at her.

A glimpse of motion jerked his attention back to the attacker. A glint of moonlight on metal—something coming at him—close—too damned close. He saw it cut through the shaft of moonlight—a shovel swung like an ax. And then all he saw was the sharp blaze of pain inside his skull. It slammed against the side of his face like the strike of lightning.

He was aware of pain. It seemed to be the chaos that

114

had been before the beginning of time, shapeless and complete, surrounding and stifling him. But slowly it twisted itself into a form.

It felt as if a bronc had stepped on his face. But he didn't think that was what had happened.

There was sound. It came like a distant rumbling of thunder from the firmament of misshapen pain. It drew closer, a threatening storm., And then it shaped into a voice that called his name.

He responded, discovering that his eyes were closed and that someone was speaking to him from close by. It was a vaguely familiar voice. He tried to look for the speaker, but his eyes didn't want to open.

The eyelids felt thick as fists. One clenched tight, refusing to move. But the other yielded, revealing a dim orange blur. As he studied it, the blur slowly resolved itself into the flame of a lantern turned very low. It barely gave form to the face that hovered near it. A familiar face, but he couldn't focus on it.

"What the hell happened?" the voice demanded.

It was Mace's voice, he realized. He tried to answer, but his mouth, his whole face, filled with pain. It flooded through him, drowning the words he wanted to form.

He figured out that he was lying on his back, and he thought to brace himself, so that he could lift up the leaden weight that was his head. But his arm didn't want to work.

God, but his head hurt.

He felt Mace's hand on his shoulder, helping. And he struggled until his arm moved. Finally, he was propped up on his elbow. Then he got the other arm working and lifted the hand to his face. The pain all seemed to radiate out from his left cheek. His fingertips touched lightly and felt. But there seemed to be no feeling in the flesh of his face except for the wellspring of pain. His skin couldn't tell where his fingers touched it.

He moved his hand away, and was aware that it was smeared with something sticky and wet. Holding it out, he squinted at it and recognized the dark stains for blood. A lot of blood. Something had sure whopped hell out of him.

"Seth, do you know what happened?" Mace was asking. He tried to answer. He tried to shape words but the only feeling in his mouth was pain. His lips barely moved. He tried again and managed an ill-formed, "Dunno."

It seemed to satisfy Mace. He nodded to himself, then asked, "Think you can walk?"

Seth wasn't at all sure about that. But he told himself he had to try. He bent a knee, dragging up the leg to get it under him. Hanging onto Mace's arm, he struggled up. And the ground began to tilt. For a moment he thought he was going to fall off, into unconsciousness. Clinging to Mace, he fought to hold onto awareness.

The spinning eased. Drawing a deep breath, still gripping Mace, he tried taking a step. To his surprise, it worked. It was his head that seemed to be the real problem. His legs functioned after a fashion. With Mace supporting him, he could walk.

He'd never realized before how damned far it was from the barn to the bunkhouse. It seemed as if he'd spent hours in slow, painful trudging before he finally reached it and Mace was helping him to stretch out on the bed.

With his head propped on the bunched-up pillow, he found the world was steadying up and the shadow-forms were taking clear shape. The pain softened into an almost bearable throbbing.

Something touched his face on the left side where he couldn't see it. Something wet and cold. Funny how anything cold could burn so. It felt like fire tracing over his cheek. He turned his head slightly, and saw that Mace was wiping at his face with a damp cloth.

"Hold still," the foreman grunted at him.

His mouth felt as if it was whittled out of hardwood, but this time the stiff lips gave nearly distinguishable form to the words he forced through them. "What happened?"

"That's what I want to know," Mace snapped back.

"Dunno," he mumbled.

Mace sighed. Then he said. "You *look* like you got kicked in the head."

"I feel like it." This time it didn't take quite as much effort to give the words shape. Maybe in a year or two he'd get back to normal, he thought. Recalling that boot slamming down from the loft, he added, "I reckon I did."

Suspiciously, Mace said. "There ain't no stock kept in the barn now."

"Wha'ever kicked me wore boots."

"You *saw* him?"

"No. Felt it. Boot." The sound of his own voice hurt his ears. He lay silent, considering. He'd have to tell Mace what had happened. After all, Mace was foreman and what went on here at the ranch was his business. At least part of it was. He set himself into what seemed like a damned long speech.

"Looked like I walked in on something. Real private. Got stomped for my mistake."

"But you didn't see who it was?"

"No."

There was another long silence. Seth was grateful for it. His head hurt and his ears needed the rest. Through the one eye that would open, he watched Mace wring pink-stained water out of the cloth.

Turning back, Mace grumbled, "Well, whoever it was, he busted you a good one. You ought to see your face."

"I still got a face?"

"Pieces of one. You're damned lucky that shovel didn't cut your head in two. It sure laid your cheek open."

Seth lifted his hand and explored his face with his fingertips again. About all he could tell was that it hurt like the devil. Seemed to be some swelling, and something caked in his hair. Blood, he guessed. His head felt almost as overgrown to his touch as it felt from the inside. Kicked and whomped and sliced up. Well, that was welcome home to the JayBar.

"What the hell were you doing in the barn?" Mace asked.

"Looking for a place to bed."

"Why in the barn?"

"Didn't want to waken you by coming in here. Figured I'd see you in the morning."

"You planning to stay around here long?"

"No. Not long."

"The old man wouldn't like it none," Mace told him. "I ain't sure he's gonna like you being here now. You shouldn'ta come. You shoulda left town straight from jail."

Seth remembered his reason for coming back. And then he recalled his excuse. He mumbled. "Had to get my horse."

Mace grunted. "Well, you ought to get it and get out before sunup, before the old man sees you."

"Maybe."

He gestured at Seth's face. "You want him seeing you like that?"

"No, reckon not," Seth mumbled. Mace was right: He wouldn't want his Pa to see him like this.

"You want to get away from here," Mace was saying. "You don't want anybody seeing you. You don't want nobody to know you were back here at all."

"Uh huh," he grunted. But he'd come back for a reason. He had to speak to J.B. before he could leave. Couldn't think it out now though. Not in any shape for thinking.

"Morning," he said. "I'll straighten it out in the morning."

"Don't worry about it," Mace told him. "I'll waken you. Get your horse ready for you. I'll see you get away all right without you run into anybody."

"All right," he mumbled. And he let that thick, heavy eyelid close.

Chapter 12

Seth woke slowly, not sure whether he'd been asleep or passed out. Some of both, he decided. He tried opening his eyes and was glad to find that they both worked. The left one only squeezed open about halfway but even that was an improvement. Blinking, he focused on the bulky form seated at the table.

Mace's back was to him. Silently he watched the way the foreman bent to pull on his boots. He moved as if he, too, were weary and aching. He'd sure aged during these past six years, Seth thought. Well, J.B. had probably leaned pretty hard on him during the time the old man hadn't had a son to rawhide. He recalled the way Mace had been before—a bull of a man, as strong and untiring as Jeremy, despite being quite a bit older.

Those two had been a lot more like brothers than ever Jeremy and he were, he thought. The both of them were big, bull-strong and almost as dark as Indians. It seemed ironic that by chance Mace was a man who had the look of a Yarborough while he, Seth, wasn't. He wondered how different things might have been if *he* had grown to that height and bulk.

If he'd really been a Yarborough—if he'd looked like a Yarborough, maybe no one would ever have questioned his right to a place on the JayBar. He'd belong here and he'd have something worthwhile, some promise of a decent future to offer Annie Johnson. Maybe he'd even still have Jeremy alive as a brother.

But what the hell was the good of thinking that way? What was done was past and Jeremy was dead. There was no changing that. No changing any of it, and the devil could take the Yarborough fortune, as far as he was concerned.

It was Lucille who'd take the Yarborough fortune, he told himself. She was using J.B., cheating on him now, and someday she'd have the JayBar and everything that went with it. Well, at last someone would be getting the best of the old man. But to his surprise he found no pleasure in the thought. He lay contemplating it, wondering how J.B. could have been tricked so. Lucille was a money-grubbing cheat who could have had no more reason for marrying him than his fortune.

Annie had said J.B. married the woman because she had a son who could be made into a Yarborough. She'd said J.B. needed a son. But J.B. didn't *need* anything. He was a man of granite, complete and self-sufficient. Whatever he wanted, his money and power could buy for him.

So the old man had bought himself a son who was no more his own blood than the son he'd run off.

Well, maybe Chuck would turn out better. But the kid would have a hard time doing it with J.B. for a father and that woman mothering him like a hen. What the kid really needed was a brother—somebody like Jeremy. Somebody who could understand what he was up against and . . .

Mace stood up, catching Seth's attention. He rose stiffly, stomping his feet down into his boots.

"Morning," Seth muttered.

Wheeling, Mace peered at him with a trace of a frown. "How you feel?"

"Like hell."

"You remember anything more about last night?"

"No."

"You still don't recall who walloped you?"

"Didn't see him."

Nodding to himself, Mace glanced toward the window. "It'll be light before long. I'll catch your horse and saddle up for you now."

Seth sat up. The move set his head to spinning. He leaned his face into a hand, mumbling, "Ne'mind. I'm not leaving yet."

"The hell! You said you'd be going this morning!"

"Said I'd *think* about it this morning."

"Look here, you got no reason to stay on, have you?" Mace snapped.

Seth eyed him, wondering what had him so randy this morning. Was he afraid there'd be more trouble with Lucille? Maybe Mace already suspected she'd been the woman in the barn last night.

Mace looked worried, and a little angry. He grunted, "Well?"

"I got a damn good reason," Seth answered. He didn't like that demanding tone of voice. He didn't want to be pushed.

"What?"

He couldn't tell Mace the truth. That'd sure rouse more trouble. Evasively, he muttered, "I feel like hell. I don't feel like riding."

Mace looked as if he could believe that easily enough. But he didn't seem sympathetic. "Maybe after you've had some coffee . . ."

Seth sighed. He had no intention of being shoved off the ranch with his business unfinished. But the idea of coffee appealed to him. He sure needed something. Shrugging, he swung his legs over the side of the bed. As he got to his feet, there was an unnerving flare of nausea in the pit of his stomach. He stood clutching the bedstead, wondering if he really was in too bad shape to ride. But the sick feeling faded. He settled at the table while Mace poured coffee and handed it to him.

It did help. The bitter heat of it cut through the fuzz inside his skull and seemed to sharpen his vision.

"Better?" Mace asked, watching him critically.

"Yeah."

"I'll saddle your horse for you."

He was beginning to get downright annoyed by the foreman's insistence. Dammit, he'd been run off this place once already. This time, he'd decide for himself when he was ready to go.

"No!" he snapped. "I told you I ain't leaving now."

Mace's hands clenched, then slowly opened. He turned away, setting the coffeepot back on the stove. Tight-voiced, he grumbled, "All right, but you get back to bed and stay there. You don't show your face outside this room, understand? I got work to take care of, but I'll be back as quick as I can."

"You afraid I'm going to tangle with the new Mrs. Yarborough again?" Seth asked.

"Yeah. That's it. I don't want you making more trouble for her. Or with J.B. either. You understand?"

He couldn't be blamed for feeling that way, Seth told himself. But there was going to be trouble whether Mace was willing or not. Somebody on this place was going to admit to trying an ambush-murder.

"Yeah," he muttered in reply. He leaned his head back to swallow the last of his coffee and for an instant the world spun. It seemed as if the chair was going to spill out from under him. Yeah, going to be trouble, he thought, but not yet. Not until he got his brains unscrambled enough to be sure he could stay on his feet. "All right. I'll go back to bed."

Mace nodded slightly. He didn't look at all happy about it. There seemed to be an anger in him that was almost too much for him to handle. He stalked out, slamming the door shut behind him.

When Seth stretched out again, it felt good to put his head down on the pillow. He closed his eyes, hoping more sleep would help. Had to get his strength back. Had to finish his business and get the hell away from this place soon.

It was midmorning when he woke and tried getting up again. This time it was easier. He dragged himself out of the bed and leaned on the bureau, studying his image in the mirror.

Mace was right—he looked like he'd been stomped. There was still plenty of blood caked on his left cheek, scabbed into a gash that seemed long, wide and deep enough to bury his forefinger in. The flesh around it was puffy and discolored. The whole side of his face seemed swollen. He touched his fingertips to his jaw, feeling the beard stubble and the tender flesh under it. Sore as hell. Be a while before he tried shaving again. Be a while before he stuck his nose into a hayloft without giving warning, too.

Dammit, that bastard could have gotten rid of him without smashing into him that way. It wasn't any of his concern what went on in J.B.'s barn—with J.B.'s wife. Just a word and he'd have left peaceably. He might even have laughed at the joke on the old man.

But he knew that wasn't so. He couldn't laugh about what that woman was doing to J.B. He hated her for it, hated knowing about it.

He asked himself what the hell it mattered to him? And what did it matter which one of them wanted to kill him? But it did matter. Unanswered, that question would gall at him for the rest of his life.

122

Wearily, he walked to the door and shoved it open. He peered out cautiously, squinting against the sunlight that knifed into his eyes. The big house loomed across the yard, dominating the ranch. Was J.B. in now? He had to confront the old man. But not yet . . .

"Mace!"

That was Chuck who'd called out. He saw the kid coming toward him, likely thinking it was the foreman who stood shadowed in the doorway.

He was sorry for that. He didn't want to see the boy now, or have Chuck see him. But there was no escaping it. He took a step back, deeper into the shadowed room. If the kid could be kept outside, the sun strong in his face, he wouldn't be able to see in clearly.

"Mace?" Chuck called again as he came up.

"It ain't Mace," Seth mumbled, remembering the way he'd used the boy for a shield when he ran from those two lawmen. He'd wanted then to try to explain. He still wanted to. But he felt as if it would be futile. And what did it matter?

The boy stopped short, frowning against the sun, trying to peer through the doorway. Uncertainly, he asked, "Seth?"

"Yeah."

"You did come back!"

"To get my horse," Seth muttered, almost apologetic.

"Is that all?" The kid sounded disappointed.

Seth nodded. "I'll be leaving pretty quick."

Chuck looked at the ground. He toed at it with his boot. Hesitant, as if he were embarrassed, he said, "Pa got a long telegram from Mister Grayling in Kansas. I seen it."

"Yeah?"

"It said there wasn't any trouble getting them to drop the charge against you. Said the feller you shot was raising hell and shooting at you. Said there were a lot of witnesses who swore to what really happened. You weren't at fault at all."

"J.B. knows that?"

The boy nodded.

So the truth had managed to leak out after all. Seth leaned against the doorjamb, feeling almost weak with relief. That had been more damned important to him than he'd realized.

"I was wrong," the boy mumbled. He kicked at a piece of rock, seeming intent on it. He had his hands jammed into his pockets, and he didn't look up as he asked, "You *got* to leave here, Seth?"

"Yeah."

"Ma says someday the JayBar will be mine. When it is, will you come back?"

"Huh?"

"I—I'd like you to. I'd like you to stay here—if you want."

"I'm sorry," Seth said.

Chuck glanced at him, puzzled. "What for?"

He asked himself the same question. Sorry for what? For not being the brother this poor kid needed? Softly, he said, "When I leave here, I'm going to settle somewhere. I'm going to start working toward some kind of place of my own."

"Where?"

"Don't know yet." He looked off toward the jagged peaks in the distance. "Mountain country somewhere."

"You won't ever be coming back here?"

"Reckon I'll be passing through—later, once I've got things set."

"*This* is mountain country. Couldn't you settle around here?"

The kid was trying to pick himself the wrong man for a brother, Seth thought. "Look here, Chuck," he said slowly, hunting words. "Why don't you make friends with Mace? He's a fine feller, once you get to know him. You two could—well—you ought to get on fine together if you'd give it a try."

"But we *are* friends."

That came as a surprise. He could remember the things Mace had said about this boy: *Damned feisty kid . . . mean and sneaky . . . spoilt rotten . . . an ornery little sonofabitch. . . .*

"But Mace ain't like you," Chuck was saying. "He's not . . . he doesn't understand."

What the hell do *I* understand? Seth asked himself. Nothing seemed to make sense anymore. And, dammit, the floor was beginning to sway again. He was getting dizzy, running out of strength. He tightened his grip on the doorjamb, but he was afraid that wouldn't be enough.

"What's the matter, Seth?" Chuck took a step toward

him, squinting hard. "What's happened to your face? You're hurt!"

He couldn't deny it. And he couldn't keep on his feet much longer. Turning, he stumbled back to the bed and slumped on it.

Chuck ran in after him. "What's the matter?"

"Nothing."

"But what's happened to your face?"

"Fell over something in the barn last night," he mumbled. He sure as hell didn't want to talk about it to Chuck. Leaning his head against the bedstead, he added, "I'm all right. Just cracked my skull pretty hard. Still a little wobbly."

The kid was staring at his face. "Is there anything I can do?"

"No."

"Can I fetch you anything?"

"Maybe," he muttered. He did feel a little hungry, and it might be food would help him get back his strength. "You think you could get me something to eat without anybody else knowing? I'd sooner J.B. didn't find out I'm here right yet."

Chuck nodded and started to the door.

Wiggling his jaw, Seth tested the soreness in it, and added. "Something soft to chaw."

After what semed a long while, Chuck was back carrying a bundle wrapped in a linen cloth. As he held it out to Seth, he admitted, "Amelia caught me in the kitchen. She sent you this. And she promised not to tell anybody you're here."

There were a pair of tall sandwiches in the bundle, along with a lidded bowl and a preserve jar full of milk. Seth grinned slightly at that, a stiff, one-sided grin. He unsnapped the wire catch, lifted the lid and sniffed at the milk. Replacing the lid tightly, he set the jar on the floor.

"Amelia said for you to drink every bit of that or she'll take a broom to you," Chuck told him.

"Well, you tell Amelia she'll have to catch me first," he muttered as he lifted the lid off the bowl. Hot stew with dumplings in it. That was a damn sight more promising than those oversized sandwiches.

"She said if you're not feeling too bad you should come up to the house and she'll fix that cut for you. If you are too sick, she'll be down here soon as her pies are out the oven."

"The hell." He didn't want more company. But she meant well, he supposed. He spooned himself a mouthful of the stew. Good stuff, and plenty of it.

"That woman thinks she's feeding a whole trail crew," he said, picking up one of the sandwiches. He held it out to Chuck. "Can I buy you lunch?"

The boy looked embarrassed. But he took it and bit into it. Somehow that seemed to reassure him. He settled himself into the chair and stretched out his legs. As he ate, his eyes roved over Seth, then went to the gunbelt looped over the bedpost. Curiously, he ran a finger along the backstrap of the pistol.

"Leave that be," Seth snapped.

The boy shot him a dark, resentful look. "I know how to handle a gun."

"Maybe. But if you put a hole through your foot with *my* gun, it's *me* J.B.'ll skin."

Chuck eased his hand away, nodding as if that was an argument he understood well enough. He grumbled, "He took my gun away from me."

"He didn't want you giving me any excuse to shoot you," Seth muttered.

"No," the boy answered with a slow thoughtful shake of his head. "He said he didn't want *me* doing anything crazy. He said you'd leave me be if I stayed away from you."

Seth swallowed another mouthful of the stew, then said, "I didn't come here looking to *make* trouble. Just to get out of it."

Chuck was staring at him in an intent questioning way that was making him downright uncomfortable. He stared back. The boy licked his lips hesitantly. "What really happened, Seth?" he asked. "I mean when your brother got killed."

He turned away from the kid's gaze. He didn't like that question—didn't like the vivid memories it jerked violently into his mind.

They'd done damn fool things, he thought. They'd made a mistake splitting up that way. He'd waited in the rocks while Jeremy went ahead to flush the buck they'd glimpsed among the trees. He'd waited there, one leg outstretched and the rifle braced against his knee, scanning

126

the woods, catching a faint scent of the deer on the breeze. Jeremy had gone to work it toward him, not spooking it but just edging it into sight.

He'd spotted it suddenly, half-hidden among the trees with the sunlight filtering through the leaves dappling its hide. *Half*-hidden maybe, but he'd seen it clear enough. He'd damned well *known* what his sights were on when he squeezed the trigger. He'd *seen* the buck go down. . . .

But it was Jeremy who screamed.

The shot had echoed. The scream hadn't. But it had rung in his ears—in his mind—for a long time afterward. Remembering, he could hear it again. And he could feel the cold shock again.

He'd jumped, letting the rifle slide out of his hands, and he'd run toward the scream, toward the sound of awkward crashing through the brush. Jeremy had staggered toward him, and fallen. The hole through the back of his coat had been very small and clean. Too small, it had seemed, to spill out a man's life.

But as he'd knelt and touched his brother, he'd known. It was already too late when he spoke Jeremy's name. He'd turned his brother's body gently, and the hand that had been clutched to the chest had fallen limply away. The bullet had come out—but not through a small neat hole.

He'd sat there on the ground for a long time with Jeremy's head in his arms. That was when he'd cried.

Someone spoke his name. It was sudden as a whipsnap, cutting sharply through the memory. It snatched Seth into a mixed awareness, suspending him between the past and the present. He looked at the boy who sat gazing expectantly at him, and he mumbled, "It was an accident."

It was all he said—all he could say. He hoped desperately that Chuck wouldn't ask more.

Chapter 13

The rapping at the door called Seth the rest of the way back into the present. He shook his head, pulling himself clear of the vivid recollection, grateful for the interruption.

"Mister Seth? Mister Charles?" she called, and knocked again.

"Come on in, Amelia," he answered.

Closing the door behind her, she stopped to eye him critically. "Mister Seth, what on earth did you do to yourself?"

"Nothing much."

"You put your head in a butter churn?"

He grinned lopsidedly. "It was too dark to tell."

"Sure is a mess." She shook her head and began to rummage into the covered basket she'd brought. Muttering, she set out adhesive plaster, scissors and other odds and ends.

"What's all that?"

"Got to get you patched up." She held out a spool of white thread with a needle stuck into it.

"I ain't a quilt!"

"No sir," she agreed heartily. "Got to patch you up just the same. Mister Charles, will you set the water to boil?"

Seth didn't like the look of this. He asked warily, "Just what is it you think you're going to do?"

"Can't leave that cut open like that."

"Why not?"

Sighing with mock exasperation, she said, "You, a cowman don't know no better. Get blowflies in it if you do."

"I'll wash 'em out with whiskey," he answered, at least half serious. His eyes were intent on her hands as she threaded the needle. "You're not stitching me up like a torn shirt!"

She turned her back to him and tossed the threaded

128

needle into the pot Chuck had set over the fire. She followed it with scraps of muslin from the basket. Then she came back and peered at his face closely. Frowning, she shook her head and clucked her tongue.

"Ain't I gonna live?" he grunted.

"How ever did you do that to yourself, Mister Seth?"

"Tripped over something in the barn."

If she believed him, it sure didn't show in her face. Glancing at Chuck, she asked, "Would you run up to the house and fetch a bit of brandy?"

When the boy was gone, she turned to Seth again. "If you didn't tell me different, I'd swear somebody whomped you with something. Like maybe a stick."

"Suppose they did? You wouldn't go talk about it to anybody, would you?"

"No sir, Mister Seth. Not if you told me not to. But you surely set a body to wonder what you're gonna do next."

"It was an accident. Honest."

"I do admire an honest man, I surely do." Her back was to him as she took the pot off the fire. She seemed almost to be muttering to herself. "Why would anybody go hit an *honest* man in the face with a stick, I wonder."

She fished a bit of muslin out of the pot with a spoon. Tossing the hot cloth from hand to hand, she shook some of the water out of it. Then—suddenly—she dropped it onto Seth's cheek.

He managed to cut short the yelp that rose in his throat, but he almost choked on it. Teeth set, he demanded, "What the hell you trying to do to me!"

She swabbed at his face with the cloth and when he winced she wrapped her other hand into his hair to hold him still. "Cowmen!" she complained. "Won't eat decent. Go busting themselves up on horses and getting trompled by cows and getting hit in the head with sticks and they don't care none. But let a body try to do a little fixing on where they bust themselves and they start raising Old Nick."

He tried to protest, but she tightened her hold on his hair. She had a surprisingly strong grip. As he squirmed, she scolded, "You keep still now! You ain't scared of a little ol' clean water, are you? Now, you hold that there."

Obediently, he put his fingers to the cloth pressed against his cheek, and she let go his hair. His scalp stung.

"It ain't just water," he grumbled. "It's *hot* water. And that's bone down to the bottom of that hole you been scraping."

She probed into the pot again and came up with the needle. To Seth, it looked about the size of a pitchfork tine, with a pigging string hanging out of the eye.

"Oh no!" he groaned, backing his head.

"If you leave that open, it's gonna heal open, if it heals at all," she said, serious now. "But clean it out and close it up and it won't hardly leave a mark."

He didn't give a damn about a scar. Not right now. And he meant to tell her so. But the door swung open and Chuck rushed in with a bottle in his hand.

"Pa's saddled up and rode out for the afternoon, but . . ." The boy's voice trailed off as he looked at the needle in Amelia's hand.

Seth was staring at it too. He could feel the tension twisting his shoulder muscles. There was a strong urge to holler rising in him. Send them both packing. Let him do his suffering and healing by himself.

Awed, Chuck asked, "What are you going to do?"

"Just a little patchwork," Amelia said.

Seth glanced at Chuck. The look on the boy's face told him he couldn't back down now. Catching a deep breath, he tried to convince himself there wasn't anything to be worried about. But even so, he was grateful for the bottle Amelia took from the boy's hand and held toward him. He let a long swallow of the brandy burn down his throat.

"Now, you put your head down and hold steady," she ordered.

He drew up his knees and leaned an arm across them to rest his head against. His teeth sunk into his kunckles as Amelia jabbed the needle into his skin.

It didn't really hurt as much as he'd expected. Not after the shock of the first thrust. But what the hell was taking so long? Seemed like she'd had time enough to sew up the whole Colorado canyon.

At last he heard her announce triumphantly, "There now. All done."

It wasn't till then that he realized his eyes were clenched shut and his lungs cramped with the breath he held. Sighing, he looked up at her. She'd snipped a piece of adhesive plaster and started toward him with it.

"Wait a minute. I want to see what you've done to me." Grabbing the bedpost, he pulled himself to his feet.

He frowned critically at his reflection in the mirror. The stripe of stitches lay across his cheek like a centipede's track. The thread was dark-stained now, standing out against the paleness of his skin. Not much color in his face. But with the dried blood all washed away and that gaping wound closed, he didn't look half as bad as he had before.

"All right?" Amelia asked.

"You sure you don't want to add on some cross-stitching or maybe sample out the abc's?" he said to her image in the glass.

She grinned. "Ain't plain old hemstitching good enough for you? I s'pose you want your initials on, maybe a little lacy tatting around the edges?"

"No thanks. I'm not much for fancy dress. This'll do just fine." He turned and picked up the bottle again, not sure whether it was the moving around or the sight of those stitches that had stirred a faint nausea in his stomach. Whichever it was, he hoped another long drink would drown it.

Chuck was staring at him from a face that looked even paler than his own. A little green around the edges, awed and admiring, the boy asked him, "Didn't it hurt?"

He took another swallow of the brandy as he considered. He'd almost snapped out *no*, but that wasn't true. What was the matter with him—couldn't he own up that he could feel pain?

He could admit it to himself, but it was hard to say out loud. "Yeah, it hurt."

As Amelia put patches of the sticky plaster over the wound, she grumbled, "Look at him. He ain't no more sick than me. Makes a poor ol' woman walk all the way down here—makes a boy fetch him dinner in bed—you gonna come up to the house for your supper, ain't you, Mister Seth?"

He glanced at the wreckage of lunch. "No, I reckon I've had done with eating J.B.'s food."

"You're not leaving *now*?" Chuck asked.

"Not yet, but right soon. I just got one more thing to take care of here."

Amelia was packing away her medicines. She shot him a curious look. And the boy asked, "What?"

Seth studied him, thinking about the chore that was still to be done, and about other things that had happened since he'd been here. And finally he said, "Chuck, what gave you the notion I come here to kill you?"

"Huh?"

The look that flashed through Amelia's eyes had fear in it. She started, "Mister Seth . . ."

"Amelia," he snapped, cutting her short, afraid that if she knew what he had in mind she'd interfere somehow. "Amelia, don't you have work to do up to the big house?"

Nodding, she folded the cover down on the basket. As she started for the door, she looked back at him. "You take care, Mister Seth. You please take care."

When she was gone, he turned to Chuck again. "What gave you the notion I meant to kill you?"

Embarrassed, the boy stared at his own boot toes. He shuffled his feet as he mumbled, "I heard it around."

"From who?"

"Around."

"This is important to me, Chuck. I want to know who told it to you."

"Mace."

"What!"

He glanced at Seth, then turned his eyes away again. "That morning after you came back, he warned me you meant to kill me. He said I had to be real careful on account I was only such a dumb kid. He said you were mean as hell."

Seth whistled softly in disbelief. *Mace?*

"Way he said it made me feel awful, Seth," the boy stammered apologetically. "I thought—he said how you'd shot Jeremy in the back and you meant the same for me and I—I thought if I was to call you—I ain't bad with a gun. I thought maybe I could take you—have a chance of it. I meant to show them I wasn't such a kid as they all think."

"Mace said I'd come here to kill you?"

He nodded, his face pinched with misery and shame. "I didn't know no better, Seth. I didn't know he'd tell me a lie."

"Neither did I," Seth muttered. It didn't make sense—unless—he thought of Lucille Yarborough kneeling in the hayloft, and of a big bulky man who smelled of horses and who'd swung a shovel in the dark. It was Mace who'd been

132

bending over him when he'd come to, demanding to know what he remembered of what had happened. Mace and Lucille? Maybe it did make sense—of a damned ugly kind.

The first day back here, she'd come accusing him of planning to take the JayBar away from her. Had she sold a story to Mace, convincing him that Seth had come to kill her son? Had she been using Mace to rid herself of the threat she figured Seth to be?

Suddenly, with a sickening certainty, Seth knew who had been behind that bushwhacking rifle. And it was as hard to take as the idea that J.B. had meant to murder him. Maybe J.B. could have claimed some justification, but *Mace* . . .

"Chuck," he muttered, not able to meet the boy's eyes, "you'd better get on to whatever you were doing."

"Huh?"

"Go on. Get."

"But Seth . . ."

"You heard me! Get—leave me be!"

He didn't have to look at the kid. He could sense the way his harsh order stung. He could sense the hurt confusion that Chuck felt as he started slowly to the door and opened it.

Dammit, this was none of it Chuck's fault, he thought. But now the kid was the one who'd suffer, no matter what happened. No way to apologize or explain, no way to tell Chuck the kind of bitch he had for a mother.

The boy hesitated in the doorway, looking back at him.

"You heard me! Get!" he snapped, and the words lashed back, stinging him too.

As the boy closed the door behind him, Seth got up and walked to the window. He watched Chuck catch a horse out of the corral and mount up, turning to ride out at a hard gallop. And he wondered if this kid tried to outride the things that bothered him, the same way he himself tried to outrun the devil.

There was no escape from the devil that plagued him now though. He couldn't show Lucille up to J.B. If he tried and succeeded, he'd be hurting Chuck. He'd be ruining as much for the kid as for Lucille. But he couldn't just turn his back and walk out on it all, either. There was a lot more to it than just the question of who'd tried to put a slug in his back. There was—what?

133

Why the hell did he care what the woman did to J.B.? He couldn't answer himself, but he knew that he did care. Only what could he *do* about it?

Maybe if he faced her and accused her—let her know he was on to her scheme and her attempted murder—well, it should upset and scare her. He wasn't sure what more he could accomplish. The only thing to do was try it and see what happened. Play the cards as they fell.

Determined, he strode across the yard toward the big house. J.B. had ridden out and Amelia would be busy in the kitchen; it should be easy enough for him to get in unnoticed and find Lucille. He went around to the front gallery. The study window was open.

As he walked silently across the deep-napped carpet, he could hear the sound of a piano somewhere in the house. Upstairs? He followed the music across the grand hall and up the curved staircase, and he found an open door.

He stood there, looking in at Lucille Yarborough. The piano was against the wall, and the window behind her spilled light into her golden hair, giving it a softness and a brilliance that was almost a halo. She was playing for herself, her hands moving slowly over the keys, drawing out a strange, sad melody. Her thoughts seemed far away.

It was the wrong kind of music, he thought. She should have been playing something triumphant and gloating, not so hauntingly wistful. He watched her, not quite sure how to begin what he wanted to say.

And suddenly she realized he was there. She wheeled, surprise flashing across her face, leaving a wary hardness. She stared at him. He knew she was taking in the bandaged cheek and the bruises, but not questioning them. Why should she? She'd been there. She knew what had happened.

"What do you want?" she snapped at him.

"Nice tune," he muttered, still not sure how to start. "Does it have words?"

She had caught her composure. Her voice was level as she said, "Yes. *Last night there were four Marys, tonight there be but three . . .*"

"What's it mean?"

A corner of her mouth twitched. "It's about a woman who was hanged for infidelity."

134.

That surprised him. He put a sharp and ugly edge onto his voice. "Is that a hanging offense?"

He could see that her cold calm was costing her effort. She asked again, "What do you want here?"

He shook his head. "It ain't going to work. I'm too ornery to die easy. You'll have to find a better way to kill me than . . ."

"What!"

She'd make a good poker player, he thought. Her startled frown looked genuine. He said, "You think I don't know you sent Mace out to put a bullet into my back?"

"The hell!" She still looked confounded.

He touched his fingers to the bandage on his face. "You should have had him finish the job last night. Nobody else knew I'd come back to the ranch. You had a damned good chance then . . ."

"I—what the devil are you talking about?"

"Don't try playacting with me! I've got the whole picture. I know you married J.B. to get your hands on his money, and you've got it. You've got this house and the fancy clothes and the good name, but J.B.'s an old man now and you're still young. You want more than J.B. can give you. So there's Mace. He's still young too, isn't he?"

"Yes! Goddammit, yes!"

"So when I showed up and you figured I was a threat to you, you sent Mace out to kill me."

"No! I never—Mace warned me about you but I—he—not killing! I swear it!"

"Your word's good, ain't it? Good as your marriage vow?"

She was on her feet now, facing him, one hand clutched on the edge of the piano. Intensely, she said, "Listen to me. There's no lie. Your father knows. He understands."

"About Mace?" he snapped in disbelief.

The hard strength in her seemed to wane. Her hand clung to the piano as if she needed something to hang onto.

"Not who or where—not openly—but he—" She paused, drawing breath, hunting words. Then, more calmly, she said, "J.B. married me for just one reason. I had a son he could make his heir. He needed someone to take over here when he's too old, and he had no one left. So he married me. And I married him for the same reason—

135

because of my son. We both know that. There isn't any question of love between us. Charles is the only thing that counts. The rest is just a business agreement."

It was an astonishing admission. He asked, "How the hell can you do it?"

"For Charles." She gazed narrow-eyed at him. "Charles is all in this world that really matters to me. I've made a home for him here and I've assured his future. You won't ruin that. I'll stop you if you try. Somehow I'll stop you."

"By murdering me?"

"I swear I never—I never even thought of it. But if I have to, Seth Yarborough, I'll *do* it. I'd kill you myself to protect Charles!"

She really meant it, he thought incredulously. She meant *all* of it. A strong, hard woman, and an honest one in her own way. All the cruel viciousness she'd attacked him with— That was her defense—she was a wildcat fighting for her cub.

"All right," he said quietly. "Look, I don't want to hurt Chuck. I don't want this damned ranch. I'm not after anything here but answers."

There was a trace of color in her face again, and its lines were softened by puzzlement. He knew that she was wondering whether there was any truth in what he'd said.

"I don't want to hurt Chuck," he repeated. Wheeling, he stalked away. Maybe she and J.B. *were* right for each other: a granite man and a wildcat woman.

But if she weren't responsible for that ambush, who could have been?

Chuck had said it was Mace who'd told him Seth came back here to kill him. And apparently Mace had given Lucille some kind of warning about his return too. Was it possible Mace really believed those things?

Seth shook his head slowly in answer to his own silent question. Mace had known him most of his life, had always been a friend. It had been Mace who'd confided things to him when he was a kid—who'd warned him about the ugly rumors—who'd prepared him for impending troubles. It had been Mace who'd explained to him that Yarboroughs always bred true—who'd told him why J.B. was raising him with Jeremy, like a brother. It had been Mace who—who had told him a few days ago that he was a damned rank sonofabitch and *always had been*.

136

He'd reached J.B.'s study and was heading for the open window. He stopped, staring at nothing, wondering. Had Mace *heard* those cruel rumors, or had be *begun* them? Had Mace been giving *warning* of trouble—or *starting* it? How many wild scrapes had he gotten into because Mace had *primed* him for them?

The pattern it made was startlingly clear. But the *why* of it was beyond him. What the hell had he ever done to earn that from Mace? What *could* he have done back then when he was just a runny-nosed kid?

Confused, shaken by his own thoughts, he rubbed a hand across his face. It was damp with sweat. As he started walking again, the carpet seemed unreal, insecure under his boots. He hoisted himself through the window and hurried around toward the corrals.

He collected his gear and roped the coyote-dun out of the pen. When he'd saddled up, he lashed his bedroll behind the cantle. He wanted to be ready to leave quick, once this was done. He wanted almost desperately to be gone and away from this place.

The voice that called to him startled him, as if waking him from a dream. He winced, looking toward the kid.

Chuck was riding in on a lathered horse, coming at a hard gallop. With a heavy hand, he brought the animal to a sharp half-rearing halt.

"Easy there," Seth snapped at him. "You'll ruin a good horse that way."

He didn't pay any attention. Eying the bedroll, he asked breathlessly, "You're not leaving? Not right now?"

"Yeah."

"Please, Seth, don't go! Not yet. Stay a while longer!"

Seth shook his head. He busied himself with tugging at the knots he'd put into the tie-strings.

"Then let me go with you!"

Startled, he looked up at the kid.

"Let me go with you, Seth. I can't stand it around here any more. Not with Pa always rawhiding me, and Ma never letting me do nothing. You're the only one who knows what it's like, Seth. Let me go with you! I won't be any trouble!"

"Like hell!" Seth rubbed a hand across his face. Turning, he leaned a shoulder against the dun and looked up at the kid. "I know it ain't easy, Chuck. But you stay here

137

where you belong. You stick it out and stand up to them. You're close on to being a man. *Be* one."

"But . . ."

"But nothing! It's no good running away. You're fit for better than saddle tramping. Someday you're going to be boss of this spread and you'd damned well better be a good one."

He swung up onto the dun then. It humped under him, taking his attention for a moment. When it had settled, he looked to Chuck again. "One of these days I'll get back by this way. And when I do, if you ain't a better man than I am, I'll beat hell out of you. You understand?"

The boy nodded, his face solemn. He looked as if Seth had thrust an overwhelming responsibility on him. He sat watching silently as Seth wheeled the dun and rode away.

Chapter 14

The ranch hands working in the back pasture eyed Seth with hostility, but they answered his questions. Yeah, they'd seen Mace. He'd been riding the big blue appaloosa, heading up toward the beaver dam.

Seth knew the spot they meant. It was a pond deep in the woods. As he came onto it, he caught sight of Mace, alone and dismounted, looking at the dam. Probably studying over what needed to be done about it before the fall rains set in. It seemed odd to see him busy at ranch work now, as if everything was right and square with the rest of the world.

Ambling the dun, Seth moved out of the shadowed woods, onto the bank. Mace looked toward him, squinting, then frowning. "What the hell are you doing here?"

"Come to talk to you." Seth's voice grated through his throat like broken rock.

"There didn't nobody at the ranch see you, did they?" Mace demanded. "I told you to stay hid."

"Why? So nobody'd know I'd come back? So nobody'd worry when I disappeared?"

"Huh?"

"Why didn't you finish killing me last night in the barn? You had your chance then, when nobody else knew I was here."

Mace stood ankle-deep in the water, his feet spread, his knuckles resting on his hips. His hat brim shadowed his face. He lifted a hand, reaching lazily to push it back. His *left* hand.

Seth flung himself to the off side of the horse.

He was quick, but so was Mace. He heard the blast of Mace's gun. Pain lashed into his thigh as he swung his left leg over the cantle.

The dun half reared, startled by the shot. It almost shook him loose from his sudden, insecure crouch in the right stirrup. He clutched at the saddle horn with the hand that held the reins, hauling them short. The horse snorted, but stood. Hanging on awkwardly, pressed against its side, Seth was shielded by its body.

His own gun was in his free hand now. He leveled it under the horse's neck. But he didn't want to use it.

"Drop it, Mace," he shouted.

But Mace just stood there in the water, his revolver dribbling smoke. He hadn't cocked it again. And he made no effort to move. He just stood there, a target that couldn't be missed.

"Dammit, Mace, I don't want to hurt you," Seth called. He meant it. He wanted answers, not blood.

"Try," Mace said calmly.

Something was damned wrong. Shifting aim, Seth let the hammer fall. He heard it snap, but nothing more. The gun in his hand was dead.

"It don't work without a firing pin," Mace said, grinning. "Took it out last night while you was asleep." His thumb caressed the hammer of his revolver, drawing it back with easy confidence.

The horse was a shield between Seth and that gun, but a living, vulnerable one. Slamming a spur into its flank, Seth let the useless weapon slide out of his fingers. He jerked at the reins as the dun started to rear, and stabbed it again. It lunged, bolting in panic at the rowel's sharp urge.

The sudden move startled Mace. His shot went wild. He fired again, and Seth was aware of the bullet skimming close. He clung to the horse's side, crouched for protection, tugging rein to swing the frightened animal into the forest.

There was no doubt left now that Mace had been the bushwhacker. It was probably Luncille's presence in the barn that had kept him from finishing the job last night. Behind him, Seth heard the hooves of the appaloosa breaking into a hard run. Mace sure as hell meant to finish it now.

Seth wanted to get himself back into the saddle, but his left leg felt made of wood and set afire. A shaft of pain was thrust through his thigh, midway between knee and hip. When he tried to move it, the pain flared, spreading through the whole leg.

He dug his teeth into his lip, filling his mouth with the

140

taste of blood. It took effort—a damned lot of it—to get his leg over the cantle. But at last he had done it and was astride the saddle again. And that hurt like hell too.

He lay low across the fork to keep from offering his back as a target, and glanced over his shoulder. Mace was lunging the appaloosa through the trees, racing hard on his heels.

The frightened dun swerved sharply around an outcrop of rock, switching leads. Seth was jolted with pain at the sudden movement, and the dun was broadside to Mace.

He fired.

Seth felt the impact of the slug—felt the horse wince under him as it was hit. Stumbling, the horse screamed. He flung himself out of the saddle at it went down. He sprawled clear of the fallen animal, but he was half-stunned, pinned by the shock of fresh pain in his leg.

Gasping for breath, he struggled to his elbows. The sound of the galloping appaloosa was close. He glimpsed it through the trees, coming up fast. Wrapping a hand around the trunk of a sapling, he started to haul himself to his feet. He made it up, but he couldn't run. Not on that shot leg. It wouldn't take his weight. And there wasn't any place to run to anyway . . .

He looked at the dead horse, feeling a moment of loss. The coyote had been a damned fine animal. And then he looked toward Mace, thinking that pretty damned soon he'd be dead himself.

He was scared. He had to admit that to himself. He stood clutching the sapling, with his weight on one leg, and a sick fear twisting in his belly. He felt cold and weak, and nigh choking on the taste of blood in his mouth.

He spat. All right, so he'd die. So he was scared—but bedamned if he'd show it. He glanced at the ground, and at an upthrust of rock near the tree. Braced with a hand on the trunk, he stretched out his hurt leg. Carefully, he lowered himself to sit on the rock. He looked at the blood smearing his thigh. He concentrated on it. Didn't seem to be a bad wound.

He explored it with his fingertips, surprised at how steady his hand held. The bullet seemed to have gone clean through, leaving a small hole where it went in and another where it came out. Well clear of the bone. Not bad at all. Nothing like the hole a bullet had made through Jeremy's chest.

He listened. He didn't raise his eyes, but his whole attention was on Mace as the appaloosa slowed to an amble. It moved in closer. Confident and curious, Mace drew rein.

Seth pried open the knot in his bandanna and pulled it from around his neck, trying to seem unconcerned about the man who gazed at him, gun in hand.

Mace stepped down. He too moved as if there were time aplenty for anything and everything. His eyes inquisitive on Seth, he said, "You're a damned cold bastard, ain't you?"

Seth wished to hell it were true. He wished his throat weren't so tight he felt about to strangle on every breath he took. Holding his hands to the job of wrapping the scarf around his leg, keeping his eyes on it too—he couldn't look up or Mace might see the fear in his face—he asked, "Why, Mace? What did I do to you?" His voice surprised him. It was calm and steady. "Why kill *me*?"

"You damned bastard!" Mace spat it out with a viciousness that startled Seth. It was too bitter, too personal. It *had* to be a hatred that had festered for years. Again, he asked himself what sin he could have committed against this man.

"All this time, all these years, that sonofabitch raised *you* like you was his own son. He gave *you* everything he gave Jeremy," Mace said, the words slithering off his tongue like a snake uncoiling itself. "But *me*—his own blood—what did *I* get? A damned cowhand's wage for doing a damned cowhand's job!"

His own blood? Seth looked up at him, astonished. He stared at the dark, strong-boned face and the Yarborough-like bulk of the man. How the hell had he been too blind to realize it before? He'd compared Mace's looks to the Yarboroughs often enough—but he'd never considered a reason for that resemblance.

None of it is *my* doing, he thought desperately. He said, "Not any more. J.B. ran me off. None of it's mine now."

"*I* ran you off," Mace answered. "*I* done it all. You never even had a notion what really happened to Jeremy, did you?"

Mystified, Seth gazed at him.

He nodded, his mouth twisting into a smug grin. And Seth remembered a shot that echoed, a scream that didn't

—or had there been two shots, so close to each other that one had seemed like an echo of the other?

"Good God," he muttered.

The delight that flared into Mace's eyes sent a chill colder than fear down his spine.

"You never had a notion, did you?" Mace said again. He looked proud of himself. "I trailed the two of you. I just watched for my chance, and you done real fine giving it to me. Then *you* took all the blame. And when I started saying as how you'd killed him apurpose, you took the blame for that, too, didn't you?"

Seth swallowed hard. Holding tight rein on his voice, he asked, "What did you do with the buck I shot?"

"Hauled it off a little ways behind some rocks and buried it. You didn't notice. You were too damned busy crying. I never seen you cry before that, even when you was real little. Never since neither. You give me a surprise then. I didn't think you had it in you. Thought you were a damned cold bastard even back then."

Seth glanced at the gun that was aimed into his face. He was afraid—but not just of dying. Suddenly there was something more important than just holding onto his life. There was the truth. Dammit, he couldn't die without anyone else ever knowing the truth. He couldn't let himself be killed with J.B. still hating him for Jeremy's death.

The words were shaping in his throat—he could feel himself about to plead for his life—he choked them back, knowing that was just what Mace wanted. He understood now that Mace wanted to see him cry again, but this time for himself. Mace wanted to know just how long he could look up the bore of that forty-five before he began to shatter and beg.

And as long as Mace held off waiting to see a sign of weakness—*that* was how long he had to live and to figure himself a way to keep living. Taut, holding onto himself with every bit of strength he had, he began to finger a knot into the bandanna around his leg.

"You ain't gonna need that," Mace said.

"Don't want to bleed to death," he grunted.

Mace laughed.

Seth hunted desperately for words to stall with. He asked, "You figure when J.B. dies, you can marry Lucille and have the JayBar yourself after all?"

Grinning, Mace nodded. "I've killed J.B.'s true son

143

and I'm gonna kill you. I've took his woman, and I'll get rid of that brat of hers. Then I'll have it all—everything he ever meant to give to Jeremy or you or that kid. And I'll have took it all from *him*."

"You really think she'd marry you?"

"Sure. I've already took her. She's a high-spirited one, needs a rider like me to handle her. She wants me and I fancy her."

"You what!"

"She's my kind of woman. Once that brat of hers is dead and gone so she ain't all the time thinking about him, she'll be plenty happy to have me make her another one."

Seth glanced at the gun again, knowing that somehow he had to get from under it. He had to stop this man, even if he got himself killed doing it.

He jerked the knot tight in the makeshift bandage. Slowly, he bent his knee, wincing as he drew up the leg. Mace was watching curiously, and Seth knew he was wondering how much the wound hurt.

He wrapped his hand around the sapling, as if he meant to stand up and test the injured leg. Mace would want to know if he could do it, would want to see if he buckled up in pain when he tried. He crouched, his weight on his good leg, as if he meant to stand. Or to lunge. It would be a damned long chance but . . .

The shot rang like sudden thunder, the bullet screaming between them. Startled, Seth paused. And Mace wheeled.

Seth saw Chuck, stepping out of the brush, with the gun in his hand still spewing powder smoke, and his face a dead, cold white. And Mace suddenly turning toward the boy, attention diverted—

"Stop it, Mace!" Chuck was screeching, his voice so thin that it snapped, the brittle edges catching in his throat. He was a kid, shaken and scared sick, but making a man's stand. And he was the instant of diversion Seth needed so desperately.

As Mace wheeled toward the boy—as the forty-five's muzzle swung away from him—Seth lunged.

The gun in Mace's hand bucked. The shot was a deafening roar so close over Seth's head. His ears rang with it. But the impact he felt was all against his shoulder— not a bullet, but his own weight ramming into Mace's legs.

144

As he stumbled back Mace jerked up the gun, trying to slam it like a club. But he was unbalanced, falling, and the blow glanced off Seth's shoulder.

Mace landed, sprawling on his back. Tumbling with him, Seth dug his right foot against the ground, shoving himself forward. He was across Mace's chest, grabbing for the gun. His hands clamped onto Mace's, trying to wrench the weapon loose.

He felt Mace's free hand ram against his side, the fist hammering into muscles that were still sore from that fight in the barn. But his grip held. He twisted at the gun. Mace was too strong though. He realized that as Mace jerked back the hand, hauling him with it. He was going to be shaken loose of his grip if he didn't do something quick.

He slammed his forearm down, across Mace's throat, leaning his full weight on it.

Mace bucked, gasping for breath, trying to roll. He writhed under Seth, flailing both legs, trying to get at him with a kick. But Seth was leaning hard on his windpipe, clamping it shut.

He could hear Mace's desperate gurgling fight for breath. He could feel the grip on the gunbutt weakening. Mace's free hand groped, prying at the fingers Seth held locked over the gun, then dropped away. And for an instant Seth thought he'd won.

Mace struck, slapping backhanded, knuckles ramming into the bandage on Seth's cheek. Lightning struck, a violent red blast of pain shooting throught his face. It blinded him, burning the strength out of him. And he was being twisted away. He felt Mace scrambling from under him.

He hung suspended in a moment of sightless nausea but slowly the pain began to ease. He knew he lay on his back, now gasping for breath himself. Blinking, he saw Mace as a blurred figured looming over him. His eyes focused on the gun in Mace's hand.

He heard the shot.

But he felt nothing. That startled him. No impact, no fresh pain. And then he realized *he* hadn't been shot.

It was Mace who staggered at the slam of the bullet. It was Mace who bent, then crumpled, the gun sliding from his suddenly limp fingers.

Seth rolled and grabbed for the sapling. As he dragged

145

himself to his feet, he stared down at the body, seeing the hole between the shoulder blades. A small, neat hole like the one that had cut through Jeremy . . . He shook his head as if he could shake away the memory. And he looked toward Chuck.

The boy stood awkwardly poised, motionless, as if frozen in the shock of some horrible dream. His eyes were dark hollows, charred into the whiteness of his face. His hand held the gun, a thin twist of smoke rising from it to spread its bitter stink on the faint breeze.

"Chuck," Seth called to him.

He didn't seem to hear. He just stood there, as still as the dead man he stared at.

Seth took a step, testing the injured leg. It bore his weight. There was pain but somehow it seemed distant—unimportant. He limped toward the boy and reached out. "Chuck?"

There was no answer, no recognition, and that was somehow as frightening as the threat of death had been. Gently, Seth closed his hand over the gun. The kid's fingers were coldly stiff on the butt. He drew the gun away from them, and suddenly they were trembling.

"I killed him!" The boy's voice was all breath, vague and uncomprehending. "I shot him—in the back!"

"It wasn't your fault," Seth said. He could see pain behind the kid's eyes. It was a damned rotten way for things to have happened. Chuck was just a boy, a lot younger than he himself had been when Jeremy died. Not likely anyone was going to accuse Chuck of murder. But still it was an ugly business to be known for shooting a man in the back, no matter how it came about. A damned ugly thing to have happened.

He looked at the gun that was in his own hands now, thinking they could go back and tell it all just the way it had happened—tell J.B. what Mace had said about Jeremy's death—but the truth would brand Chuck as Mace's killer. He could damned near hear the gossip: *Got his first man when he was sixteen—got him in the back.* And how would J.B. react? How would Lucille feel about it—her own son had killed her lover? What would *that* do to the boy?

Chuck just stood there, dazed and shaken, staring at the corpse.

It was bad enough here and now, Seth told himself. It

would be a damn sight worse back at the ranch. He asked himself just how important cleaning up his own name really was. Hell, he'd expected to live out his life with the guilt and accusation of Jeremy's death. He'd got by for six years. And now he knew he was free of the guilt. Did he *have* to rid himself of the accusation too—at the boy's expense? It wouldn't bring Jeremy to life again.

The truth was what people wanted to believe, despite whatever really happened. He owned that he would have killed Mace himself. He'd meant to. Why couldn't that be the truth? Who would it hurt? What was one more killing against his own name? It couldn't hurt him—not the way it would Chuck.

He put a hand on the boy's shoulder, asking, "Do you hear me?"

Chuck nodded slightly.

"*I* killed him. You're going to be my witness. That's what you're going to say happened."

"No." The boy shook his head slowly, his gaze still fixed on the body. "You didn't shoot him. I did it."

"It was *my* doing," Seth said.

The kid faced him then, though the stunned eyes seemed to look past him—through him. "No. He's shot in the back. Folks would say you murdered him."

"Not if you back me up," he insisted. "You tell them we fought for the gun. Tell them he rolled over just as it went off. Something like that. They won't hold me to blame if you tell them that." The wasn't quite true, he thought as he said it. They'd damned well hold him to blame. He just hoped nobody took a mind to hang him. Well, if that happened, J.B. would get him out of it, wouldn't he?

He held the gun toward Chuck. "You clean this when you get home. Then put it away. J.B. told you not to wear it. You forget that you did."

The boy took the gun. He turned it in his hands, staring at it, and Seth knew that he was still dazed by what had happened.

Gently, he asked, "You understand?"

The boy nodded.

"Then you catch the horses, will you?"

Obediently, he moved to take up the reins of the appaloosa, then went off to find his own mount.

Seth took a step, feeling the wound in his leg more

as a numb ache than as pain now. He was able to pick up the gun Mace had dropped and slip it into his own holster. When Chuck came back leading both horses, he was able to walk enough to help lift Mace's body and lash it behind the appaloosa's saddle. Then he hauled himself up onto the horse and, with Chuck at his side, turned back toward the JayBar.

Chapter 15

They rode silently, swinging around to come up to the mansion from the front. It wasn't quite dark yet when they reached it. A twilight stillness hung in the air. The mansion loomed in silhouette against the brilliant colors of the dying sun, with squares of lamplight marking two windows. Seth picked the one upstairs as Lucille's room. The other, below, was J.B.'s study.

How long ago had he ridden up here the first time, riding in weary and hunted, looking for refuge? It seemed like years—painful years that had smoldered and burst into flame in his hands. A damned fire that had burnt them all. It had destroyed Mace and reached out to mark the kid who rode at his side now.

He glanced toward Chuck and found himself thinking of Jeremy. Sometimes a man's bloodlines didn't seem to matter at all. He and Jeremy had been brothers as sure as if they'd shared the same blood. And this boy, who wasn't really a Yarborough either, was J.B.'s son now. But Mace, who had been of the Yarborough blood and Jeremy's brother by right, hadn't been either in fact. It was strange—too damned strange to be understood.

They drew rein at the iron post by the steps and Chuck looked toward him questioningly.

"You go up to the window and call J.B. out here," he said. "Don't talk. Just call him out. I'll tell him."

Nodding, the boy stepped down and looped his reins over the post. He headed up onto the gallery, moving as if he were still lost in a dream.

Seth shifted in the saddle. Striding a horse made that damned hole in his leg hurt. He eased his good leg over the pommel and slid down, taking his weight on it. He leaned against the horse's shoulder, weary as hell, as he watched Chuck rap at the window.

It took a few moments, an exchange of soft-spoken

words that he couldn't quite make out. Then the boy was coming back. And J.B. appeared at the front door.

The old man looked first at Seth, then at the limp body tied behind the saddle. Facing Seth again, his voice level and emotionless, he said, "Mace?"

Seth nodded.

J.B. stepped back, into the shadows. He became a shadow himself, a bulk looming in darkness. In the same steady stony voice, he asked, "What happened?"

Seth's own voice was thin, but cold and unfeeling. "I shot him."

Chuck had started down the steps. He halted suddenly, as if he'd been jerked back on a sharp rein—as if he'd abruptly wakened from his dream. "No!"

"Chuck!" Seth started, meaning to cut him off. But the boy began talking excitedly, anxiously, tumbling out the words as if nothing could stop him.

"Seth didn't shoot Mace! It was *me* that done it. Mace meant to kill Seth and I *had* to do it. I shot him in the back. But I had to stop him from killing Seth."

"Shut up, dammit!" Seth was shouting, but the boy paid him no heed. And J.B. held up a hand, as if to turn back the sea and gesture a dry path through it. That upraised hand was a command that stifled Seth's protest. He knew that J.B. would hear the boy out, no matter what.

"Tell me all of it," the old man said.

Chuck drew a deep breath, trying to calm himself. He began, "Seth was leaving here and I went to follow him. I took my gun and a fresh horse and I went after him . . ."

"Why?" J.B. interrupted.

"I *wanted* to. I'd sooner go with him than stay here. I followed his tracks. Then I seen him riding fast through the woods—running, with Mace chasing after him. I meant to catch up. Then I heard a shot. I couldn't figure what was happening. I seen through the trees that Seth's horse was down, and he was on the ground. I seen Mace going toward him with a gun. I didn't understand, so I left my horse tied and I walked up quiet through the brush. . . ."

The boy stammered into silence. And J.B. turned, as if he looked to Seth for the rest of it.

It was futile now. But with a dogged determination,

Seth said, "What he seen was me fight with Mace. And kill him."

"No!" Chuck took a step down, toward him. "*You* didn't kill Mace. You didn't kill Jeremy either. I heard Mace say . . ."

"*What!*" J.B. snapped.

Chuck looked up at him. "Mace killed Jeremy. I heard him say as how he tracked them into the woods and when Seth shot a buck, *he* shot Jeremy and put the blame on Seth. I heard him say that and—and—things about my Ma and me." He hesitated, catching at his breath with a gasp that was almost a sob. For a moment he gazed at the ground. Then he lifted his head, facing J.B. again.

"He said he meant to kill me too. I was scared. I was bad scared and I couldn't do anything. Not till I seen he was really going to kill Seth. Then I shot. Not at anything, just meaning to stop him. But then him and Seth were fighting and he was winning and he got up with the gun. He would have shot Seth right then. There wasn't anything else I *could* do!"

J.B. was silent, motionless, a shadow within shadows. Seth stared toward him, wanting desperately to see the old man's face. He wanted to know if there was anything in it—anger, sorrow—*anything.*

"That's the truth of it, Pa. I swear it," Chuck added, his voice soft against the twilight stillness. He stood straight, his head up, his eyes steady on the old man.

Quietly, J.B. said, "Charles, take Mace to the bunkhouse. Get a couple of the men to take him inside. Seth, you come into the house with me."

He turned then, striding through the doorway without waiting for any reply, as if he didn't doubt obedience to his orders.

Couldn't he feel *anything*, Seth thought as the old man disappeared from his sight. Couldn't he sorrow for a dead son? Or pride himself in a boy turning man? Didn't he *care?*

He glanced toward Chuck. The boy still stood on the steps, looking at him inquisitively, as if it were *his* place to give the orders and answer the questions.

He nodded, holding out the appaloosa's reins. "Do like he said. Take Mace to his own quarters."

Chuck took the reins, leading the horse away. And

151

Seth looked at the open door again. He could make out the dim figure inside. J.B. was waiting there for him.

He wiped a hand across his face and drew a deep breath. Then, cautiously, he took a step. The hurt leg bore his weight. He started up the stairs, fighting desperately not to limp—or to show any sign of weakness. J.B. was watching him.

The old man led him on through the darkness of the house, into the study. The lamp on the desk was turned low. As J.B. reached to raise the wick, Seth snapped, "Leave it like that."

The old man's hand hesitated. In the flickering of the dim light, it seemed to tremble. Then, to Seth's surprise, it drew back, leaving the flame low.

He'd voiced an order—and J.B. had complied. Had that ever happened before? It gave him a feeling of uncertainty. He didn't know what to expect next or how to defend himself.

Stiffly, he sank into the winged chair and stretched out his legs. He crossed them at the ankles, hoping to hell J.B. wouldn't notice the crude bandage on his thigh. He didn't want to admit the injury.

The lamp was on the desk and J.B. turned to stand with his back to it, his face lost in shadow. He always did that, Seth thought, and suddenly he wondered if it might be on purpose. Was J.B. using the light and darkness to hide his face? But why should he do that? What would a man of solid stone have in his face to hide?

"You're hurt," J.B. said.

"No."

"I'll get Amelia to bring in her medicines. She . . ."

"No!" Seth insisted. Dammit, he didn't want help.

J.B. hesitated, poised as if he argued some question inside himself. Then, in a voice like gravel, he said, "Tell me *why* it happened, Seth."

"That was what it came to. Chuck wasn't a part of it. Me and Mace—one of us had to kill the other one. I done it as sure as I'd had the gun. That was what it came to."

They'd all been damned from the start, he thought. Every one of them—Jeremy, Mace, himself. Now maybe even Chuck. All of J.B.'s sons were damned.

He heard himself demand, "What did you want of a son? Jeremy was dead. Nothing could change that. I

152

wasn't good enough—not even your own son. Nothing could change that either. But Mace had your damned Yarborough blood. He was your son every bit as much as Jeremy. Why didn't you accept him?"

"*You knew?*"

"He told me. When he was about to kill me, he told me."

The old man shook his head slowly. "I didn't think he knew."

Seth's hands knotted themselves. The habit was long-built and ingrained. The deep feeling in him twisted, turning on itself and shaping into anger. "What the hell did you want from him? Why didn't you make *him* your son?"

"I didn't think he knew," J.B. repeated dully. "I brought him up here from Texas. I meant to do right by him. I gave him a job and a home here. I made him my foreman . . ."

Mace's words were still vivid in Seth's mind. He snapped, "*A damned cowhand's wage for a damned cowhand's job.* Sure, you gave him work, but that's all you ever gave him. You never made him your *son.*"

"Seth," the old man said, his voice quietly tight, "Mace was the bastard child of a half-breed whore. . . ."

"And not good enough to have the Yarborough name? You gave it to me. But Mace was *your* son—with *your* blood. What the hell did you want from a son?"

"I don't know." The old man seemed as if he meant to say more, then changed his mind. Then, changing it again, he said, "What did I ask of *you*, Seth?"

"Huh?"

"You're my son. . . ."

"Like hell!"

"I raised you for a son. I treated you the same as Jeremy. I gave you everything I gave him."

"Sure!" Seth gazed angrily at the shadowed face, wishing he could see what lay in the old man's eyes. "Yeah, you kept me to measure Jeremy against so you could look every day and see for yourself how much bigger and better a Yarborough was than some common brat. You gave me everything you gave him so you could compare us and see how much better he did with a thing than I could!"

"Good God, Seth, you're near two years younger than Jeremy. I never expected you to match him."

"Like hell you didn't. All the presents you brought us—identical handguns, but *wasn't* it a contest to prove he could learn to shoot faster and better than me?" It hurt as he said it. But it was like the hot water Amelia had scrubbed into the wound on his face. With the pain was a sense of cleaning out dirt that had festered against his bone as long as he could remember. "And the horses, as close-matched as any fine harness team, only *not* so he could prove fair that he was the better rider?"

"Nobody ever measured you against Jeremy," J.B. answered. "Nobody except you yourself. Seth, you were damned young when you began to hear talk and have suspicions I wasn't your true father. And you were always broody-natured. If I'd given Jeremy anything I didn't match for you, what would you have thought my reason was?"

Startled, Seth turned his face away from the old man's shadowed gaze. The answer was so damned obvious—why the hell hadn't he ever thought of that before?

It had been Mace—*Mace* who'd first suggested that J.B. intended a competition between Jeremy and himself. Over and over, Mace's words had set them against each other. How much of it all—how much of *his* life—had been shaped by Mace's scheming?

He sat silent, overwhelmed by the realization. And from somewhere deep within the hollow stillness of the house, he heard footsteps. They were distant and muffled, but hurrying closer. Sharp, rapid steps of a woman's feet rushing toward the study.

He looked up as J.B. opened the door. And in a moment, Lucille Yarborough stepped into the room.

She paused there, framed by the doorway, her face gashed into streaks of light and shadow by the low flame of the lamp. Its reflection made sparks in her eyes as she gazed at Seth.

What hell did she mean to let loose on him, he wondered. It was obvious she knew what had happened. She knew he'd killed her lover.

But when she spoke, he realized it wasn't Mace she meant. "You think you've succeeded? You think you've really hurt him. You think you'll drive us out. . . ."

She was the wildcat crouching at her lair, snarling at

154

the intruder who threatened her young. It meant little that Mace was dead. Her son was the only one who really mattered to her. That was what she'd said, and Seth knew it was true.

"No!" he snapped back at her. "No, dammit! Chuck's all right. He's good stuff and it ain't his doing or his fault that he's messed up in this. He don't deserve trouble for it. *I'm* to blame for the killing."

She looked as startled as if he'd slapped her. She'd been ready to claw and scratch—to fight to the death if she had to. But he wasn't challenging her. The lines of her face softened into a vague puzzlement. She glanced uncertainly at J.B. and he nodded.

She turned to Seth again. "You—you mean that. Charles told me, but I didn't believe him. You *really* meant to protect him!"

"Lucille," J.B.'s voice was strangely gentle—a way that Seth had never heard it before. The old man reached for his wife's hand. "It's all right, Lucille. No one—nothing—is going to hurt Charles."

She faced him, her hand closing over his. And Seth knew that Lucille Yarborough had been wrong when she'd said there was no love between herself and her husband. There was a kind of understanding between these two that he wouldn't have thought possible to either of them.

He sank deeper into the chair, lost in his own confusion. The whole world—everything he'd believed in—was like a heat mirage, twisting and changing shape in front of his eyes. The cold, emotionless man of granite spoke tenderly to a wildcat woman whose eyes were suddenly moist and gentle.

"Lucille," J. B. said as if it were the first word of much he meant to say. And he stepped through the doorway, drawing her with him, into the darkness of the hall.

Seth could hear the murmur of their voices, but not the words. He could heard the gentle and comforting tones. There was an understanding between these two. . . .

He glanced toward the window. The sky beyond it had gone completely dark. An evening breeze tugged at the curtains, fluttering them, bringing in the cool scents of the mountains.

There was no anger left in him now. There was nothing to hide himself behind. He felt naked, defenseless, and somehow shamed, as if it had been *he* who'd brought

155

these troubles to the JayBar. *He* was the intruder here.

Leaning heavily on the arm of the chair, he stood up. The wound in his leg was a sore ache, but not pain enough to hold him here. It bore his weight. He limped across the carpet, his spurs making a ragged jangle. He had to seat himself on the windowsill to swing his leg over it. That was when he looked back, into the empty room. Only the shaggy head of the buffalo was familiar. And its glass eye seemed to gaze at him without recognition. All the rest of it, the walls, the furnishings, the damned soft carpet, were strange. None of this was a part of *his* life.

He turned his back and stepped onto the gallery, into the night. The moon hung low, like a broken disk of white ice, spreading its frosted light over the clipped lawn and the forests beyond. It showed him the lone horse standing head-hung, dozing at the hitch post. Chuck had taken the appaloosa around, but had forgotten his own horse.

The kid needed somebody to teach him proper respect for an animal, Seth thought. But he was grateful for a saddled and ready mount.

He started toward it, and the pain in his leg spilled out with a sticky warmth. He realized the wound was bleeding again. All that moving around had loosened his makeshift bandage.

Mumbling a soft curse, he limped to the steps. He seated himself stiffly, stretching out the sore leg, and jerked loose the bandanna.

"Seth?"

Startled, he looked back over his shoulder. J.B. was leaning through the open window, then climbing out and coming toward him. He bent to busy himself with the scarf. He wasn't sure he could face the old man again.

"Seth?" J.B.'s voice sounded strangely small out here in the night.

"I'm taking a horse. No hundred dollars this time, just a horse." He nodded toward the dozing animal at the hitch post. "That one."

"Now?"

"Yeah."

"Where will you go?"

"I don't know." He hadn't meant to answer. It just slipped out. He was silently cursing himself again.

"Mace is dead," J.B. said slowly. "And Charles is still

too young . . . Seth, I need somebody here on the ranch to run things for me."

"Huh?" He looked up, not quite able to believe that the old man meant what it sounded like.

"I'm asking you to stay here."

The tangle of emotion he felt was raw and frightening. He recoiled from it, twisting it into resentment, into protective anger. "Six years ago you told me to get the hell off your land."

"That was a long time ago, Seth. It was—I was—I didn't understand then."

"You mean you thought then that I had *murdered* Jeremy. Now you know different, so all of a sudden I'm the prodigal son returned? Like hell—I'm still the same—"

"I *never* believed you killed Jeremy intentionally."

"You ran me off for it."

"No." The old man spoke hesitantly, as if he had trouble finding and shaping the words he wanted. "Not for *that*. Jeremy was dead, and I needed you. I *needed* you then, Seth, but you turned your back on me. You behaved as if you didn't care. For a time I thought maybe you didn't. You acted as if you were glad Jeremy was dead."

"Glad!" Seth repeated incredulously.

"I was wrong. I know that now. I've seen you with Charles, and he's your brother now, isn't he? Not another Jeremy, though. He's *you*. You look at him and you know he needs you the same way you needed Jeremy."

It was true, Seth thought. And he was amazed that J.B. could have known and understood.

"You and Jeremy needed each other. And I needed you both," the old man continued. "I still need you, Seth."

With hands that were no longer steady, Seth tightened the bandanna and began to work a knot into it. His eyes were on the bandage, but it was his own thoughts that he saw. This man who spoke to him now was a stranger to him—not the cold man of stone he's seen all his life—but a man of flesh and feeling like himself.

That granite face had been a mask. J.B. hid behind it, the same way he himself hid behind flaring anger. J.B. rode a tighter rein than he did, holding cold and hard most of the time instead of going off half-cocked at every touch. He knew now, though, that J.B. *felt* those touches, those proddings and pains.

157

It was startling, bewildering, to realize that it was just as hard for the old man to speak out his feelings as it was for him. Right now, talking this way, the old man was baring his own soul and hurting as he did it.

And suddenly, as if he couldn't stand it any longer, J.B. snapped, "Goddammit!"

Seth looked up at him and asked softly, "Goddamn what?"

"You! You're a short-tempered, mule-headed, stiff-necked, mean-natured brat. And I'm a short-tempered, mule-headed, stiff-necked, mean-natured old man. Blood or no blood, you're my *son*. I want you to stay here. I *need* you here! Can you get that through your damned thick skull?"

Seth began to laugh. There was nothing funny in it, but he couldn't help himself. *This* was the J.B. he knew, shouting and ranting and ready to whip him into obeying.

He pressed his face into his hands, laughing until he was breathless. Then, glancing at the old man's puzzled face, he found his voice again. "We fight, don't we, Pa? We fight and you run me off. You order me to stay and we fight."

"Maybe I should stop giving you orders," J.B. said.

Seth shook his head. "It wouldn't work, Pa. We'd keep right on fighting."

"What's wrong with that. You fought all the time with Jeremy, but you'd always make it up again."

"Jeremy was my brother. We understood each other."

"I'm your *father*, dammit! Can't *we* learn to understand each other?"

The knot in the bandanna was already tight. But Seth jerked at it, sending a shock of pain through his leg. He *knew* what he wanted. For the first damned time in his life, he *knew*. He wanted to stay here and be a son to this man. It was what he'd always wanted, but he hadn't understood that before. Now he knew and now—he'd never been able to speak out the really important things—and now he couldn't do it. He could shape the words in his mind, but his mouth wouldn't say them.

He jerked at the knot, hating himself for his own damned inability. If only Jeremy were alive, he thought desperately. Jeremy had been able to understand things without having to have them spelled out in so many words. Could anyone else understand in that same way?

"Pa," he said tentatively.

The old man was looking at him, waiting tensely for an answer.

He couldn't say it. Instead, groping, he muttered, "Hell, Pa, I can't leave now. I promised Annie Johnson I'd take her to a dance Saturday."

For a moment the old man looked bewildered. Then his shoulders stiffened and the corners of his thin, hard mouth twisted slightly, hinting at a grin. Almost casually, almost as if he were just making conversation, he said, "You think you're going to be able to dance on that leg?"

There was a sense of relief. It washed over Seth, overwhelming him. He caught at his voice and answered, "I'll damn well try."

"You're just stubborn enough to do it." J.B. held a hand toward him. "Come inside and I'll get Amelia to fix it up right for you."

Accepting help was admitting the need of it. That was hard. It was one of the hardest things he'd ever done—taking J.B.'s hand, leaning on the old man's shoulder and accepting his help back up the stairs, into the house. But he did it, and he felt a strange sense of accomplishment in it.

"There's a real fine dance just before Christmas you might want to take her to," J.B. was saying.

Seth understood that it was a question. Christmas was a long way off. J.B. was asking him again, this time in his own kind of roundabout terms, to stay on the JayBar.

And this time, in this way, it wasn't so hard to answer. "I always liked the shindigs after spring roundup myself. I reckon I ought to plan on taking her to that, too, come spring."

Lee Hoffman was born in Chicago, Illinois, and attended Armstrong Junior College in Savannah from 1949 to 1951. During her first college year she discovered science-fiction fandom and the vast network of correspondence and amateur publishing that it supported. She made many friends in this new world and even founded her own monthly magazine, *Quandry*, which attracted an enthusiastic audience. In addition to her interest in science-fiction, she continued to be an avid Western fan. Finally, in 1965, she completed a book-length Western of her own, *Gunfight at Laramie* (1966). Shortly after this first Western novel was accepted, Hoffman was commissioned by Ace to write a comic Western. It became her second book, *The Legend of Blackjack Sam* (1966), a novel all about "the Notorious Showdown at the O'Shea Corral." The years of writing for the amateur press and her own amusement were now paying off. *The Valdez Horses* (1967) is perhaps her masterpiece. Its emotional impact, aided by a surprise twist in the last line, make this novel difficult to forget. It received the Golden Spur Award from the Western Writers of America. In other novels such as *The Yarborough Brand* (1968) and *West of Cheyenne* (1969), no less than in *The Valdez Horses*, character and motivation are as important as details of the plot. It isn't that Hoffman skimped on action—there are fistfights, gun battles, and chases, but they serve the story rather than being the story's reason for existence. Hoffman refused to be predictable. In common with B. M. Bower before her and P. A. Bechko after, Hoffman tried her hand more than once at comic Westerns, notably in *Wiley's Move* (1973) and *The Truth About The Cannonball Kid* (1975). R. E. Briney in the second edition of the *Encyclopedia of Frontier and Western Fiction* concludes that Hoffman has always had "an enviable command of the writer's craft and the storyteller's art."